PERSONAL ISLANDS

For Dee
Whose constant support and belief
makes all things possible

Thanks also to
Bruce Colman, Dr James Mair,
David Robinson, Dr Rachel Wells, Holly Yorston
and especially Dr Nick Oliver
who taught me more about my pancreatic duct
than I ever thought I would want to know

Crumps Barn Studio
Crumps Barn, Syde, Cheltenham GL53 9PN
www.crumpsbarnstudio.co.uk

Cover design by Lorna Gray © Crumps Barn Studio

Printed in Gloucestershire on FSC certified paper by Severn, a carbon neutral company

ISBN 978-1-8382298-9-4

MICHAEL BARTLETT

PERSONAL ISLANDS

FAREWELL MY LONELY and other stories of solitude

Crumps Barn Studio

Your life is an island separated from all other islands
and continents. Regardless of how many boats you
send to other shores or how many ships arrive upon
your shores, you yourself are an island separated by
its own pains, secluded in its happiness

Khalil Gibran

We live, as we dream – alone

Joseph Conrad

A note from the author:

I first wrote these stories in 2011. Since then, we have had the COVID 19 pandemic where many more people have had isolation thrust upon them, so now seems a good time to finally publish them.

It is customary to state that no characters in these stories are based on real people. As usual that is true, though some – though by no means all – of them are based on various aspects of people I have met.

So, to all my family, friends – and enemies –

don't bother looking. You are not here.

Though of course, if the cap fits …

A SEPARATE PEACE

The Isle of Purbeck

It was 6.40 on a sunny May evening. The older man looked round his sitting room, plumped up a cushion and returned a book to its proper place on a shelf. He stood there for a moment in thought. He had not sought this meeting, he did not want this meeting, but his natural courtesy meant that he had to welcome his two imminent guests with politeness. He ran his fingers idly over the keys of the Baby Grand that stood in the bay window. Almost automatically he took out his handkerchief and wiped a finger mark from the polished top next to Margaret's photo.

It was 6.41 on a sunny May evening. The woman walked slowly along the footpath through the meadow that led towards the old farmhouse on the side of the hill. The wind was light and she caught the fleeting scent of wild mint. She was uneasy about this meeting. He had sounded very courteous on the phone and had agreed to see them but she sensed reluctance.

It was 6.42 on a sunny May evening. The younger man swung his car round a tight bend, relishing the way it held the road without much slackening of speed. The sheer aerodynamics of the car pleased him, the top was down and the whisk of the wind past his head was curiously comforting. He was excited about joining this protest group. It would give him the chance to shine locally and, if this evening was successful – as he was sure it would be – he would also be working with someone famous, or at least well known, someone who had achieved so much. Maybe there'd be a bit reflected glory. He eased off slightly on the throttle and began to peer forward, looking for the entrance to the lane.

It was 6.43 on a sunny May evening. The lanes and fields of Purbeck looked much the same as they had done for hundreds of years. A wire fence here, a telegraph pole there, the loose macadam of the road surface, all minor modern additions. The trees, the hedges, the fields, the wind, the faint tang of salt on a southerly breeze, the piercing cry of the swifts high above, the warning chatter of a robin defending its territory. Always the same, year after year, season after season.

But for how long?

It was 6.50. In his sitting room in the old farmhouse, the older man heard the rasp of tyres on gravel and smiled. He'd had a private wager with himself that the younger man would be the first to arrive. As careful in his retirement as he'd been all his professional life, he'd taken the trouble to explore the background of his two expected visitors.

The younger man was a partner in a firm of estate agents in Poole, early thirties, married, eager, no time to waste. He would be conscious of his status in the firm, the older man thought – conscious, perhaps over-conscious, of the unprepossessing background he'd managed to outgrow. Probably unlikely to have much patience, unlikely to see the virtue of a measured approach to any problem.

The woman on the other hand was more reserved. She came from this part of the world originally but had only moved back here from London a year or so ago after the early death of her husband from cancer. She'd given up a lucrative job as finance director with an advertising agency in the West End and now – from the sublime to the ridiculous – earned a little cash by doing the books for a number of small local firms as well as helping with the financial management of several charities.

He was curious about why the protest committee had chosen these two people in particular. The younger man he could understand. He would be providing a lot of the initial impetus for their group.

In fact, this visit was probably his idea. But he was less certain about why the woman was coming, although he was glad she was. There was always less chance of a confrontation when there was a third person present.

They had not actually told him the specific reason for their visit, but he knew. All those years in the various corridors of power meant he never went into any situation unbriefed. He read the papers, watched the news like anyone else. A couple of quick calls to London – one to a retired Brigadier – a drink one evening with a friend on Purbeck District Council and he already knew far more about the situation than, he suspected, either of his visitors did. But that wasn't the issue here. He would let them make the running.

6.52. The woman emerged from the footpath and stepped onto the gravel forecourt of the house. She smiled faintly when she saw the car in front of her, long, sleek with too many fins for good taste. She had timed her arrival perfectly – she hadn't wanted to be the first here. She crossed the gravel to the front door and rang the bell. Glancing back as she waited, she saw a kestrel hovering high above the neighbouring field. Hanging on the wind, endlessly patient, knowing that the process could not be hurried but that, given time, his evening meal would appear.

The Virginia creeper held the front of the house

in its embrace. The evening smell of the stone spoke of many years in this place. The silhouette of the trees in the east, a faint sound of sheep from several fields away, no sound of traffic, no sound of the 21st century. She loved this part of the country. The door opened. She stepped forward into the house.

7.10. The initial courtesies were over. The older man had offered drinks and now the woman was sitting on a leather sofa holding a glass of very dry white wine. The younger man sat beside her with a single malt with a dash of soda. The older man's slight wince at the request for soda had not gone unnoticed by the woman. He was sitting opposite them, his whisky – neat – in a glass by his side.

The younger man spoke first. "What a delightful room."

The older man glanced round for a moment. "I find it peaceful. I've reached the age where I value my comfort."

"Nice piano. Do you play?"

"No …" A brief hesitation, noticed by the woman, unnoticed by the younger man. "It was my wife's. She played almost every evening."

"I can pick out the odd tune. Had piano lessons as a child but never really kept it up."

The older man smiled faintly.

The woman said nothing but she watched the

older man's face and the thought came to her. *He knows why we're here.*

The younger man put down his glass on the occasional table beside the sofa and leaned forward.

"Thank you for seeing us, Sir Richard. I think it's time I explained why we've come."

The older man nodded, smiling. "Please do."

"Well, it's like this. Mary and I are part of a committee, their representatives if you like. It's actually a protest group and it was formed to...."

His voice droned on, too much explanation, over-selling their importance on the committee. It was probably the same way he would talk to a young couple desperate for somewhere to live while extolling the virtues of a modern shoebox where the five year old plaster was already peeling off the walls.

Once or twice the older man glanced across at the woman and she met his eyes. He smiled faintly and turned back to the younger man. After five minutes or so the older man lifted one hand in a small but significant gesture that even the younger man could not fail to recognise. He stopped talking.

The older man nodded his acknowledgement. "Thank you, Mr Redfern—"

"Oh, do please, call me Malcolm."

"—Thank you, Malcolm. I think I have the picture." He glanced sideways at the woman, including her in the interchange.

You cunning old sod, she thought, *you had the picture long before we even came up the drive.*

Aloud she said, "Malcolm has outlined the current situation, Sir Richard, but he hasn't actually said why we're here."

"I was coming to that," said the younger man.

Watching the older man's face, the woman said, "I don't think there's any need, Malcolm. I think Sir Richard knows."

The older man's eyes rested on hers for a moment as if acknowledging a more worthy opponent. Then he said, "Let me see if I understand the situation. Your committee ..."

But the woman cut in, courteously but firmly. "And I think that not only does Sir Richard know why we're here, but he's already made his decision. Am I right, Sir Richard?"

The younger man, taken aback, looked from one to the other of them, knowing that something was going on between them but not understanding what.

The older man didn't answer the question but repeated his earlier statement. "I think I understand the situation. You have learned that the MOD is planning to sell off the South Holme Estate after all these years and that the scheme on the table at present is that they have a buyer—"

"An unscrupulous buyer," interrupted the younger man.

"A buyer," continued the older man firmly, "who is willing to pay a lot of money but whose plans include a large-scale holiday complex on this site. Not surprisingly there's considerable local opposition to this plan and your group has been formed to fight it—"

"We will fight it and we will win ..."

"I am sure you will fight it and fight hard – but who will win depends on many factors, not the least being how your committee defines a 'win' in this context."

"'Win' means defeating this holiday complex proposal."

"Which will then be replaced with another proposal. If the MOD wish to sell, they will sell. The only question is to who and for what purpose."

"But do they have a right to sell? This was never their land, they just took it during the war." Even the woman was surprised by the vehemence in her voice.

The older man nodded. "A good point, but I doubt it's a simple one to prove. I suspect there'd be a lot of argument and a lot of lawyers will get very rich before that is settled."

"But we can't just hope this threat will go away." The younger man was becoming vehement in his turn. "Our group was formed to represent people who live here on Purbeck. We don't want this holiday complex. We know it won't be easy to fight a body like the MOD, we know it's going to cost a lot of money. And that is why—"

"That is why you and Mary—" The older man turned to the woman. "Forgive me, may I call you Mary?" She nodded.

"—That is why you and Mary have come here tonight to ask me to join your committee and to become its chairman." He looked from one to the other of them. "That is why you are here, isn't it?"

For once the younger man was almost lost for words. "Well ... yes ... but ... but how did you know?"

The older man shrugged. "Given my, shall we say, wide experience and high profile career, it seemed a logical, if slightly egotistical, deduction."

"Well, yes, that is why we've come. Having you on the committee, even better, having you as the figurehead, would make a huge difference. You know how these pressure groups work – you have influence, you know who to approach. You're just the person we need. Everyone thought so, didn't they, Mary?"

The woman nodded.

"Thank you," said the older man, "that's a great compliment."

"But you're going to say 'no', aren't you?" said the woman.

The younger man looked at her in amazement, but the older man permitted himself a wry smile. "You're very intuitive, my dear. Yes, I'm afraid I am going to say no."

"You knew what we were going to ask, didn't you?"

"I must confess I did have an inkling."

"Was there anything we could have said that would have persuaded you to say yes?"

The older man thought for a moment. "I'm not sure. Probably not, but one can never be certain. You've come to me because you think I can help. You are obviously sincere and you deserved the chance to make your case and I needed to find out if I would have the strength to stand by, knowing that I could help. One can't help feeling responsible."

"But I don't understand." The younger man was clearly totally confused by the direction the conversation had taken. "You do realise the implications of this proposal, don't you?"

"Oh, for heaven's sake, Malcolm," said the woman, "of course he does."

"The proposed link road to this holiday complex will go right past this house. You might even have a compulsory purchase order on part of your land. Do you really want this to happen?"

The older man shook his head. "No, I don't …"

"Well, then …"

"But you have to weigh the different factors in any situation and for me – and I emphasise I'm talking about me – the risk of this development, the possible road, traffic and so on, has to be set against the effort required to challenge it. For me the cost is too high."

"We're not asking you for money. All we want is—"

The woman interrupted him. "Sir Richard isn't talking about money."

"Well, what does he mean by 'cost' then?"

"I mean the emotional cost, the cost of time, the draining cost of preparing arguments, presenting them, waiting for the results, handling the disappointments." The older man smiled mischievously. "Perhaps even the cost of thinking you've won only to find you've been gazumped, and I am no stranger to that experience, I can assure you."

He paused, lost in thought for a moment, then pulled himself back to the present. "No, I'm sorry, but I'm no longer prepared to pay that price."

"So you'd rather see the whole area destroyed."

"No, given the choice I would not. But in spite of what you might think it is not a clear-cut argument. A development of that kind would bring holiday makers into this region, would provide income and jobs for local people ..."

"Oh, that old argument ..."

"Yes, that old argument. I'm not saying I agree with it but it can't be dismissed out of hand."

"But it's a smoke screen! A lot of those jobs would be temporary. Once the place is built many of them will evaporate and we'll be left with concrete, crowds and chaos."

The older man looked at him thoughtfully for a moment, recognising a conscious alliterative line that had been used before, and no doubt would be trotted out many more times before the campaign was over.

He explained patiently, "But there will also be a number of jobs for local people, plus all the visitors who'll be drawn into the region. It could be a significant boost for the local economy."

"A boost we don't need."

"A boost you don't need," said the woman.

The younger man looked at her in surprise. "I don't understand you, Mary. You don't want this development to happen either."

"No, I don't. But there's no point in fooling ourselves. It's no use pretending we're the good guys in white hats riding to the defence of this area against the barbarian hordes. There is another point of view and, although it's not mine, we have to recognise that it's a valid one and treat it with respect."

"Respect." The word was snapped out contemptuously. "They want to destroy a beautiful piece of countryside and you speak of 'respect'."

"But not everyone will see it as destroying something. They'll see it as creating something new that will benefit a lot of people."

The younger man looked at the woman as though seeing her for the first time. "I'm beginning to wonder why you're on the committee. Sounds to me as if you've gone over to the enemy."

"There is no enemy. Can't you see that? There's just another point of view."

"Why haven't you said all this in committee then?"

For the first time the woman seemed flustered. "I … I don't know. I suppose I haven't thought about it before. This threat came out of the blue, and we responded to that threat. I suppose all I could see was the need to fight. I hadn't thought about … Oh, I don't know."

The older man came to her rescue. "You hadn't thought about tactics. You saw the problem and reacted instinctively."

She glanced at him gratefully. "Yes, I suppose that's true."

The younger man would not let her off the hook.

"So you haven't had second thoughts, then? You haven't changed sides?"

"Oh, for heaven's sake, Malcolm, don't be so stupid ..."

The younger man flushed at the contempt in her voice.

"... Of course I haven't changed sides. I'd be devastated if this area was swallowed up in a development, but I think Sir Richard is right. We're not going to get anywhere by shouting loudly. We need to be more subtle – we need a plan."

"We need to make our presence felt. That's why we hoped that Sir Richard ..." The younger man tailed off.

"—Would give us some credibility," the woman supplied. "Stiffen our backbone. Gain us some publicity."

"Exactly. At the moment we're just ... oh, I don't know, voices in the wilderness, I suppose." He looked at the older man hopefully. "You wouldn't have to do much, Sir Richard. Just having you on board would help such a lot."

The older man shook his head. "It doesn't work like that. All the reasons you want me are all the reasons why I couldn't simply take a passive role. I don't wish to be unkind, but if this builds into a full scale confrontation who do you think the press will approach? You or me? Who will be required to do the public speaking? Whose photograph will they use? Who will they want to hound for soundbite after soundbite at the public enquiry? I'm sorry, it's not possible for me to take a passive role – and I do not want to take an active one."

There was a moment's silence, then the young man drained his glass. "Well, that's that then." He stood up. "Sorry to have wasted your time."

The older man glanced at the young woman and saw her distress at the lack of courtesy. He paused, then his expression changed. His one-time colleagues would have recognised that he'd made a reluctant, but necessary, decision.

He made a gesture with his hand. "You haven't wasted my time, and for heaven's sake sit down, Malcolm. Don't let your pride get in the way of common sense."

Surprised, the younger man sank back onto the sofa.

"I will not become actively involved," said the older man, "but I will give you some useful advice."

The younger man opened his mouth but the woman silenced him quickly.

The older man paused for a moment, gathering his thoughts. "You do need to expand your committee," he said, "not just in numbers but in terms of people, different backgrounds, different areas. At the moment, if I'm right …"

Of course you're right, thought the woman, *you've done your homework very thoroughly.*

"… You have a committee of five people, the two of you, two landowners and a local business man."

"Well, yes, but how …?"

"You need to expand that, you need more variety, local trades people, farmers, young people, more women, you must be able to demonstrate that you speak for everyone in the area, regardless of background."

"But you said yourself that not everyone will agree with us."

"Of course they won't, but you can't be an effective pressure group if you only represent a narrow interest. So, secondly, you need a strong chairperson – of either sex – and before you say anything" – again he held up his hand in the gesture that precluded interruption – "there are other good figureheads. Apart from me. You just need to find one."

"Easier said than done."

"We never thought this would be easy," said the woman.

"Then you need to map out a strategy, that's essential when planning any kind of battle. My main suggestion here is – avoid all negatives. Don't be against something, be for something."

Now it was the woman's turn to look puzzled. "I'm not sure I quite understand."

"It's quite straightforward. Don't openly oppose the holiday complex. Accept the fact that if they've actually taken the decision, then the MOD will sell whatever happens. Your job is to find and promote an alternative and then to get public opinion on your side."

"What sort of alternative? Any building project is going to destroy this area."

"Why does it have to be a building project? This area has been wild for years. Ironically, the fact the MOD have used it as a firing range may not have been good for local visitors, but it has helped preserve a wide variety of wildlife."

"Oh, I see," said the younger man, "we need to find a colony of crested newts, do we?"

For the first time that evening the older man laughed out loud. "I like that, Malcolm. Not an original solution, but you're right in principle."

The woman nodded. "You mean we could approach someone like a wildlife trust or a heritage body to see if they would buy the site for conservation."

"Something like that. It may need to be an ambitious project of its own to defeat the holiday complex but it's worth exploring. The point is if you come up with something along those lines you'd be fighting for a positive, not a negative and that makes a huge difference."

The younger man nodded. "I see what you mean."

"And finally, or finally for this conversation anyway, you need a good Press Officer or PR person."

"Yes, we may have someone who'll take that on. He used to be the editor of his village magazine before he moved down here and ..."

"Forgive me, but I think you need more than that. Does your committee have any funds at its disposal?"

"Some, and we have a promise of more."

"Then I suggest you try and recruit a professional. It's not a full-time job and you might be able to do a deal with them. But you'll be much better off with someone who knows their way round the national media world and, more to the point, someone who is known to the media. They will make sure your message is heard and heard in the right places."

"But where would we find such a person down here?"

"Doesn't have to be down here. You need someone with the professional skills who would also be sympathetic to your cause. I might be able to help you there. I'll make a couple of calls and give you a ring next week."

"Well, that's wonderful, Sir Richard, you've been

very helpful but won't you …?"

The older man held up his hand. "No, that will be it. After that, I am, as the young people say these days, out of here."

He stood up and it was clear that the interview was over. The younger man got to his feet.

"Well, I can't say I'm not disappointed, but we do appreciate your suggestions. We'll certainly take them back to the committee."

The woman nodded.

"Right then, Sir Richard, I'll say goodnight. You coming, Mary?"

"In a moment. I'm going to walk back anyway." She turned to Sir Richard. "I wonder if I might just use the bathroom before I go."

"Of course, it's just down the hallway."

Five minutes later with the snarl of the younger man's car still faintly echoing on the evening air, the woman came back into the room to find the older man standing by the piano.

"Thank you," she said. "Thank you for being so patient with us."

"Not at all. I wish you every success."

"Yes, I think you do, so I'm still not entirely certain why you won't help us. Oh, I know what you told Malcolm and I can see why our campaign doesn't have much appeal for you …"

"No, it's not that."

"Isn't it?"

The older man was silent for a moment. Then he said. "Why did you leave your job in London to come back here?"

"How did you know …?" She paused for a moment. "I presume you also know about my husband then?"

He nodded.

"Well, I could say there were too many memories in London but that's only partly true. We both had demanding jobs and when there were two of us that was fine, we fed off each other's energy. But then when Paul died …"

She broke off and he said gently. "You suddenly realised you were tired."

She looked at him. "Yes, that's exactly it. It didn't seem worth it any more. I didn't need to go on earning at that level so, well, I came back here."

"And got caught up in this fight."

"Yes. I didn't want to go on working at the same intensity, but I found I still needed to do something."

"Hence the book-keeping jobs and now this committee."

She shook her head, laughing in spite of herself. "You really are something, aren't you? Is there anything about me you don't know?"

"Yes, of course there is. We never know other people fully, no matter how close our relationship or how good our research. I've been in exactly the situation you describe but I'm older than you and there comes a time when you don't want that involvement anymore."

"And you've reached that point?"

"Yes. I have."

"I understand, and yet however much you want to retreat from the world, the world goes on impinging, doesn't it?" She gestured at herself and then the empty space where the younger man had been. "Can you really just sit back and let these things happen around you?"

"Yes, I can. Of course the battles go on, they always will. But not for me. Have you ever thought about when it is time to decide to stop – not give in – just stop?"

She didn't answer, so he went on, "Some people might decide to do it earlier in life. They choose to step down from the Parish Council, coaching the local youth football team, chairman of the chess club, whatever it might be. More likely these decisions come after a lifetime spent serving on committees, managing many teams, helping shape policy in whatever area their expertise lies, fighting many battles, winning some, losing some. One day they realise they've had enough. Perhaps they've decided they want to travel more, develop their garden, learn how to paint, be free to visit friends whenever they want. They want the rest of their time for themselves, however long or short that may be. It doesn't mean they're unsympathetic to the challenges that present themselves, but they feel they've served their time. The battles go on, but it's time for someone else to take up the fight … That's how I feel. You might say that I've negotiated a separate peace."

She was taken-aback for a moment. "But what will you do? Will you really be content simply to vegetate here?"

"I would not be content to vegetate, as you put it, but that's not what will happen."

"So what will you do?"

The older man was silent for a moment. Then he moved forward and his hands caressed the top of the piano again. He touched a key and the pure note echoed round the room.

"When Margaret, my wife, was alive," he said slowly, "she would play the piano most evenings for an hour or so. Chopin, Mozart, songs from the musicals we once went to together. Often, I was out or away, but when I was at home it was a great joy to hear her. She was a good pianist without being brilliant, but the sound of the music she played spoke of home, of quietness, of peace, of …" His voice broke slightly for a moment. "Of love … I miss that."

There was a long pause then he went on. "I will never vegetate. I am going to learn to play the piano, I'll never be any good but it will give me satisfaction and occupy my mind. Apart from that there are all the books …" He indicated the shelves behind him with a sweeping gesture. "All the books I've been intending to read for years and have never had the time. Now I have the time, however long that might be, and I do not propose to use it sitting on more committees, however worthy the cause."

There was a silence in the room. Finally the woman spoke. "I'm sorry if I have intruded on your privacy."

The older man shook his head. "You have not intruded. I only speak of things I care about to people I wish to speak to. I feel you may be one such person."

"That's a very generous thing to say."

"I mean it." He turned back to the piano. "I think you would have liked Margaret. I know she would have liked you. Will you come and see me again?"

"I would like that very much."

"No committee talk, mind. I meant what I said about that."

"I know you did."

"You see, when you live alone at my age, there is a tendency – to be resisted for the most part – to think more of the past than the present. Being conscious of roads one has not taken, that sort of thing. However, there's no real point in looking back, the 'might-have-beens' can only be destructive."

He turned suddenly and walked rapidly across to the bookshelves. "I've just started on the Russian classics. Do you know Dostoevsky?"

"Not very well, but I love Chekov."

"Good. Next time we'll talk books." He held out his hand. "Thank you for coming, Mary."

It was 8.29 on a beautiful May evening. The low, sleek fin-obsessed car was cooling down in the double garage attached to the four-bedroom house with ensuite bathroom, sharing the space with a small saloon, the sit-upon mower and a range of other unused, but expensive, pieces of garden equipment. Inside the house, the younger man was giving an exaggerated and edited account of the evening to his wife over a mug of instant coffee.

It was 8.30 on a beautiful May evening. The sun was sliding gently towards the horizon but the air was still warm. The woman walked down the drive and, before turning off onto the footpath, glanced back towards the house but the front door was already shut. She supposed that, on paper, the evening had been a failure, but she felt exhilarated. Like the man in the house behind her, she was not really lonely but there had been an emptiness. Perhaps, as a result of this evening, that emptiness might begin to recede. She walked on briskly towards the dusk.

It was 8.40 on a beautiful May evening. Ever a tidy person, the older man had already washed his visitors' glasses and they were ready to go away. He thought back over the evening. The outcome of the business part had gone more or less as he had expected, indeed as he had planned. But the woman had been a surprise. From the moment she had walked in he had sensed an empathy that he thought had gone from his life for ever. That was why he had unbent slightly and given them some guidance. He was a man who valued friendship and he thought perhaps that a new one was just starting to emerge.

Smiling slightly to himself, he poured another single malt – neat – and taking down *Crime and Punishment* from the bookshelf he settled himself in his favourite chair.

It was 9.45 on a beautiful May night and a barn owl glided silently over the unspoilt fields of Purbeck in search of supper.

Farewell, My Lonely

The Aisle of Capri

'Twas on the Isle of Capri that I found her
Far away where the sky meets the sea...

I found myself humming this old song as I arrived at our meeting place. This was the sixth week, our sixth meeting and, well, I'm probably just a silly old fool, but I felt a real surge of excitement that I would shortly be seeing her again.

I parked the car in the usual place and paused for a moment. The sun was beating down, I could feel the heat on my head and for a moment I was tempted to reach back into the car for my hat. But all I had was my baseball cap with the slogan: *"I'm a lumberjack and I'm okay"* which didn't seem quite right for a romantic tryst.

Not that it was a romantic tryst. Not really. Or at least only in my imagination. The first week we had met by chance, both in the same place at the same time to perform the same task. A small collision, no damage, supermarket trolleys don't dent easily, no-one hurt, but it had led to a brief conversation and a smile.

And what a smile. It made her whole face light up. It was a smile that reached out and touched you, a smile that you somehow felt had been created just for you; it sort of folded you in as though we were partners in a hostile world and had just found each other. The sort of smile that made you want to rush home and watch *Casablanca* for the umpteenth time.

The sort of smile that, in spite of yourself, made you wonder ...

Our second meeting was a week later, same place, same time. As I've got older I've noticed a tendency, which I'm not sure I really like, to let the routine things in my life fall into a pattern, to do certain things at certain times on certain days. So I do my ironing on a Sunday evening while watching the *Antiques Road Show*. I have my breakfast at eight o'clock while listening to the *Today* programme. I mow the lawn on Saturday mornings and so on and so on.

Not that I think it matters having regular habits, just so long as they don't take over your life. Some months ago, I was invited out to Sunday lunch with friends who live about thirty miles way the other side of Redhill. It was a nice lunch, good conversation, very relaxing and then towards the end of the afternoon I caught myself thinking: *I'd better go soon or I'll miss the Antiques Road Show and I won't get the ironing done.*

Fortunately, I realised how silly that was. I stayed on and later we all went down the pub together, but it was a nasty moment. I became very aware of just how easy it would be to let a sensible routine become a rigid habit. Now I sometimes do the ironing on a Tuesday morning instead, just to break the rhythm as you might say. It's very odd. I've felt pretty restless since Jill died but somehow that restlessness has developed into lethargy. There's no one who, out of the blue, might suddenly say, "Let's do so-and-so", and without that spur it's very easy to take the line of least resistance and do nothing.

Anyway, back to our second meeting. This was as unexpected as the first but it was one occasion when I was glad that my rigid habit had brought me to the same place at the same time on the same day. I recognised her at once – how could I not – and this time I got the smile without the need for the collision first and my heart lifted. She remembered me.

To be honest our conversation was brief. We reminded each other of how we'd met in the same place last week, inevitably we exchanged comments about the weather. And that was it really. I would have liked to have complimented her on the dress she was wearing but I thought that was a bit forward on our second date, sorry, I mean meeting.

There was no excuse to linger and we both had things to do, but just as I was preparing to move off she suddenly said, "Oh, I wonder if you would mind … the spaghetti up there … I can't quite reach."

"I'd be delighted," I said and stretching up, took the packet of spaghetti off the top shelf and handed it to her.

"Thank you so much," she said and once again that smile lit up the world. "The top shelves can be so difficult when you're as short as I am."

"Short, but lovely," I said, I hope gallantly rather than patronisingly, and this time the smile was accompanied by an impish grin.

"You're too kind, sir," she said with a kind of mock curtsey, and she trundled her trolley off towards the tills.

I have always enjoyed the company of women, more so than of men, although I have plenty of friends of both sexes. Not that I am a philanderer – I wouldn't want you to get the wrong idea. I've only been married once, very happily, and when Jill died, well, I just didn't feel like marrying again. I may be silly, but I felt as if it would be like replacing her with a newer model and that was the last thing I wanted to do. But it's lonely without her and although I'm never short of people to meet, things to do, I miss the ebb and flow of everyday conversation.

I don't mean Jill and I spent all our time discussing Jean Paul Sartre or the state of the economy. It was more on the level of "Where are the scissors?" or "Have you fed the cat?" That's not what I miss. I can find the scissors for myself and the cat soon lets me know if I've forgotten to feed her. It's not the practical things; it's knowing someone else is there. It's being able to share anything that happens, big or small, good or bad. It's the ability to spot something unusual on the telly, or see a beautiful sunset or find a funny passage in a book and be able to say: "Did you see that?" "Isn't that beautiful" or "Just listen to this."

I don't have that any more.

That's what loneliness is.

And you're always wondering if there's an answer while knowing, deep down, there probably isn't. But it doesn't keep you from wondering.

And so that is why, when this woman first smiled at me and then a week later I saw her again, my silly old bus-pass mind just wondered. That's all. Wondered …

Ah, well …

And I can still see the flowers blooming round her
Where we met on the Isle of Capri.

Our third meeting – same time, same place – I like to think was anticipated by both of us. To be honest I was running a little late so, although I had other shopping to do, I broke my ordered routine, skipped the fruit and vegetables – I could do those later – and went straight to Aisle 7, the aisle where they kept all the pasta, pizza bases, tomato sauce toppings and other things Italian. As I hoped, she was there and once again that lovely smile lit up her face.

"Well, I don't know," she said, "this is becoming rather a habit, isn't it?"

For the first time I wondered how old she was. Younger than me, that's for certain. Maybe ten years younger, early fifties perhaps. You could knock another five years off when she smiled but there was something about the set of her face that made me think she was older. And there was another thing. Suddenly the thought came to me. She has known great pain, but she has coped.

I caught myself up short. Amateur psychologist now, was it? Almost certainly reading too much into too little. Time to come back down to earth.

"Can I reach you any spaghetti, ma'am?" I asked.

She laughed, "No I'm fine for spaghetti today, thank you. Perhaps I should always plan my meals from things stored on the lower shelves."

My meals, I noted, not our meals.

"That's fine," I said, "until the supermarket indulges in its customary little games and moves everything around. That could play havoc with your diet."

"What makes you think I'm on a diet," she said and I suddenly realised how my light remark might have been interpreted.

"Oh, I'm sorry ... I didn't mean—"

My embarrassed apology was cut short by her snort of laughter. "Don't be silly. I'm teasing."

I sagged with relief. "Oh, yes, I see. Of course."

"Well, I'd better get on," and she pushed her trolley forward and got it entangled in mine, just like our first meeting.

"This really is becoming a habit," she said. "I hope you've got comprehensive insurance."

"Never venture into a supermarket without it," I said solemnly and she laughed again.

We disentangled our trolleys and she began to move away.

"Well, goodbye, until our next collision."

I suddenly took my courage in both hands. "I wonder, could I treat you to a coffee ... When you've finished your shopping?"

She hesitated and for a moment I thought I'd

spoiled everything but then she nodded. "All right. About twenty minutes? I'll see you in the café."

I raced through the rest of my shopping, letting my customary care go hang. No time today for detailed price comparisons, I just wanted it done and dusted.

Even so she was there ahead of me, sitting beside her full trolley working her way through the itemised bill.

"Just like to check it," she said in response to my raised eyebrow, "they're pretty good here but mistakes can happen."

I went and got a couple of coffees – she turned down the offer of a cake. "Remember my diet," she said mischievously, and suddenly the conversation ground to a halt.

I was desperately searching for something to say when I glanced up and caught her eye. She grinned. "Tricky, isn't it?" she said, "you could try 'do you come here often?'"

"I know it's silly," I said, "but, well, we don't even know each other, do we?"

"Well, that's easily sorted," she said promptly, "I'm Helen."

"And I'm Nicholas."

"Hallo, Nicholas."

"Hallo, Helen."

And we solemnly shook hands across the table.

"Good, that's sorted," she said, "Now then, do you come here often?"

I laughed. "Once a week normally and, yes, before you ask, almost always at the same time. I've become rather a creature of habit."

"Nothing wrong with a good routine," she said, "so long as you don't let it rule your life."

A lady after my own heart. She was very easy to talk to and we chatted about this and that for about a quarter of an hour before she said she had to go.

"Same time next week?" I said cheekily as we parted.

"Probably," she said, "I know it might not seem like it but my routine is that I don't have a routine. I never know for certain until the day itself."

And on that enigmatic note we parted.

The following week, she wasn't there and I was surprised and a bit disturbed by how disappointed I was. However, just as I was pushing my trolley back to the car, I met her coming the other way.

"Difficult day," was all she said to my unspoken question but she spared 10 minutes for a coffee before she began her shopping and I went home.

On the surface our conversation was as relaxed as it had been the week before but I could sense a tension in her and finally I asked if she was all right.

"Not entirely," she said, "it's been a bad day and I haven't managed to shrug it off yet."

She said nothing more so I asked. "What is it that you do?"

"Office work," she said, "well, mostly …" and left it at that so I took the hint and changed the subject.

Summertime was nearly over
Blue Italian sky above
I said: "Lady, I'm a rover,
Would you listen to my song of love?"

The following week we nearly didn't meet at all. Just as I was getting ready to leave for the shops I had a phone call from Amy, my youngest daughter who lives in Scotland, with the news that she was going to have another baby. I was delighted, of course, and she was clearly in the mood to chat so I didn't have the heart to hurry her along. I had a quick grin to myself imagining her response if I'd said something like: "Can't talk now, darling, I've got a date with someone called Helen in a supermarket café."

By the time she'd rung off and I'd promised to go and visit them later in the year, I was running well behind my usual time. I told myself it didn't matter, that the precise time I did the shopping was not important and anyway routines were meant to be broken, but even so I had a sense of disappointment.

I went anyway, apart from anything else I was almost out of cornflakes, but as I had feared there was no sign of Helen in Aisle 7 or anywhere else. I did my shopping in what I fully realised was an unjustified bad mood which was not helped when I got home by the realisation that after all that I had forgotten to buy the cornflakes.

The next morning, I felt very restless. Lots of things to do, no interest in doing any of them. Everything seemed too much effort. I have often felt like this since I lost Jill and it's a hard feeling to fight. The best remedy is usually go back to bed with a good book, but I'd promised to meet Bill for a drink at lunchtime so I'd probably have a nap when I got back and there's only so much sleeping a man can do.

I was feeling quite scratchy to be honest so having breakfasted off the dusty remains at the bottom of the cereal packet, I decided I'd pop into the supermarket for some more cornflakes on my way to the pub. I had planned just to pop in and out quickly but on my way to Aisle 9 where the cereals were kept I glanced down Aisle 7 and saw Helen, stretching up to try and reach the top shelf.

I drew nearer and said: "Can I reach you any spaghetti, ma'am?"

She swung round in surprise. "Oh, Nicholas. What are you doing here? It's not your day, is it?"

"Not normally," I said and told her about Amy and the forgotten cornflakes.

"I didn't think I was going to see you this week," I finally said, "but it seems you weren't here yesterday either."

She shook her head. "No, I had a funeral to go to."

"Oh, I'm sorry. Anyone close to you?"

"No, not really. Oh, look, Nicholas, I really can't stop now. I'm already late for a meeting. I just popped in to grab a few bits and pieces."

Ah, well, I thought, *it was sweet while it lasted.* But rationalise as I did, there was still a slight tug of sadness.

"Of course," I said aloud, "I quite understand. Work must come first."

There must have been something in my voice because she paused for a moment and looked at me. Then she laid her hand on my arm.

"I really do have to go and there really is a meeting …"

"Of course, there is. I didn't think—"

"But I will be here at the usual time next week. Will you have time for a coffee then?"

"I most certainly will."

"Good. I'll see you next week then." And she was gone.

And now it was next week and I was heading across the supermarket car park to our sixth meeting, grinning like the silly old fool I was.

She was there, as promised, in Aisle 7 and I was able to reach up and get her spaghetti for her just like the second time we had met. The smile was still there but somehow she seemed distracted and suddenly all my excitement drained away. She's realised what I've always known, I thought, that this was a casual acquaintance that had gone too fast. Fun at first, it was no longer welcome and now it was time to end it. We parted, slightly awkwardly, agreeing to meet in the café when we'd finished our respective shopping.

She whispered softly: "It's best not to linger."
And then as I kissed her hand I could see
She wore a plain golden ring on her finger.
'Twas goodbye on the isle of Capri.

She still seemed abstracted as I put the coffees down on the table and for a moment we made polite, inconsequential conversation as though this was the first time we'd met. I knew there was something Helen wanted to say but I didn't want to rush her. Finally she came out with it.

"I'm sorry about last week, Nicholas, but I'm glad we were able to meet today."

"But you want it to be for the last time?"

Her head jerked up in surprise. "No. No, that's not what I was going to say."

"Oh," I felt my cheeks going red.

She reached across and touched my hand. "You mustn't misunderstand this but I've enjoyed meeting you. I know we still barely know each other but I feel you're someone I can trust."

'Trust' hadn't been the word I was half hoping for deep at the back of my mind but 'trust' is good, it's a compliment. Sometimes trust can be better than love.

"But," she went on, "there is something I wanted to ask you. It's just that now I'm here it seems a bit of a cheek."

I recovered some of my composure. "Why not just say what you want to say and we'll take it from there."

"All right." She took a deep breath. "I wanted to ask if you would come to a funeral with me, next week. Tuesday."

"A funeral?"

"Yes."

"Another one?"

"Another one."

I opened my mouth to say something flippant but thought better of it. However, Helen had noticed and her impish grin appeared.

"I bet you're thinking something like 'she's getting through her friends a bit fast', aren't you?"

I grinned back and nodded. "Well, yes, something like that."

Her grin vanished and her brow furrowed slightly. "No, it's not a friend, no-one I know actually."

"Oh, I see."

"No you don't. How could you?"

"No, you're right. I don't see. But clearly this is important to you so why don't you explain."

"Thank you, Nicholas."

She picked up her cup, swirled it round for a moment and put it down again. "Well, then. I think I told you I work in an office ..."

"Mostly ... you said."

"Yes, mostly. In actual fact I work for the District Council. It's a bit of a hotch-potch job, in a way I suppose I'm a kind of trouble shooter. I sort out all the bits and pieces that go wrong and especially all the bits and pieces that no-one else wants to do."

"And one of those things is to do with funerals?"

"In a way," she paused. "You've probably never thought about it but in a town this size there are a surprising number of people who die alone. Completely alone. No family, no friends, not even any interested neighbours."

"Are you talking about the homeless, those living

on the streets? There's a number of them in cardboard boxes under the railway arches, aren't there?"

"Actually, no, I don't see many of them. They may be living rough but they've often got some kind of connection with a hospital or hostel or the Salvation Army or something."

"Oh. Well, who are we talking about then?"

"Those who are really alone, usually the elderly. Sometimes they've been dead for some days, even weeks, before they're found. Once they *are* found a funeral has to be arranged, and if there are no friends or family, then that job comes to me."

"What do they die of? Starvation?"

"No. More likely an illness that's gone untreated or just even old age. Many of these people have money, but for whatever reason have chosen not to spend it. One funeral I went to last winter was for an old lady in her seventies. She had her own flat but never left it. In fact she hardly ever left the living room. She ordered basic groceries over the phone and left the money in an envelope on the step. Her neighbours said they hadn't seen her for years. The house had central heating, but it wasn't on. She apparently got flu and died of hypothermia."

"Aren't there grants for people like that?"

"People like what? She had money. Several thousand pounds actually. No, she'd just shut herself away for no apparent reason. And then she died. Apart from the vicar I was the only one at the funeral."

"But that's terrible."

"It's sad."

"And you have to go to their funerals?"

"No, I have to arrange the funeral, that's my job. I don't have to go. I just can't bear the thought of them dying alone and then being buried alone. So I go. Sometimes there's a neighbour or two there as well, but quite often it's just me."

Instinctively I reached out and took Helen's hand. "And this funeral next week, the one you want me to come to. That's another one like this but I guess with a difference, yes?"

She left her hand in mine and smiled. "I was right. You are a sensitive man. Yes, this one's different. This is a young woman, probably in her early twenties. She hanged herself in one of those flats over the other side of the park."

I was silent. I thought of Amy in Scotland, my other daughters, Julie in Canada, and Kate in Norwich. Two married, one with children and all, as far as I knew, happy. I felt the tears come behind my eyes.

"Do you know why she did it?"

"No idea. We don't even know who she is. She'd

been in the flat for a month, paid 3 months' rent in advance but she gave a false name and false references. Looks like she didn't want us to know who she was."

"And it's her funeral …"

"Yes. I'm sorry to ask you, Nicholas, especially as I hardly know you, but I don't think I can face this one on my own and I feel I must go. I keep thinking, what if it had been my daughter."

"I quite understand. Of course I'll come. In fact I'm honoured that you asked me."

She was as sweet as a rose at the dawning
But fate hadn't meant her for me,
And though I sailed with the tide in the morning,
Still my heart's on the isle of Capri.

I sailed on no tide in the morning, of course, but perhaps my heart, or at least part of it, is still in Aisle 7, the aisle of the Italian delicacies, where I first reached down the spaghetti for a woman I did not know.

I went to that funeral with Helen. We stood side by side in the crematorium as a young girl, remembered only by a name that wasn't hers, left the physical world for ever. Apart from the vicar and the men from the funeral company, Helen and I were the only people there.

As Helen had said, I was struck by the sadness,

not the death as such – that's an inevitable part of living – but the dying alone, unacknowledged, unmourned.

I have been to three more funerals with Helen since then. No more young people, thank goodness, but still people who in those last moments of life had no-one. We cannot change that, Helen and I, but we can make sure that there is someone waving farewell as they set out on their final journey.

It is very sad. And yet I feel, oh, I don't know, fulfilled I suppose in an odd sort of way. For the first time since Jill died I feel as though I have a purpose. Someone needs me. Oh, not Helen. Although our friendship is deepening I know that is all it will ever be. No, I mean those who had no-one, no-one at all, not even someone to say that last goodbye. We say that goodbye, Helen and I, and it brings me peace.

It also makes me smile sometimes to remember that I once thought I was lonely.

BECAUSE HIS MOTHER CAN'T

The Falkland Islands

I t was not a particularly difficult journey, but it was a long one. Every year sometime in mid-May she would pick up the phone in her little stone cottage on the edge of Bodmin Moor and order a taxi to take her to Plymouth. At Plymouth she would sit quietly on the platform for about twenty minutes – she always liked to leave herself some spare time – before taking the train to London.

At Paddington she would transfer to the Heathrow Express arriving at the airport in time for a light meal before catching the evening flight to Madrid. When she arrived, she would walk slowly through the maze of corridors to a distant part of the airport where she would check in for the overnight flight to Santiago.

Her routine was well established. On her arrival in Chile in mid-morning she would engage the services of a taxi from one of the booths inside passport control. This, she had found with experience, was the cheapest and most reliable method of reaching her hotel. On arriving there she would re-book the same cab for the following morning, sometimes this was an official booking, sometimes the driver did her a private deal. She didn't mind which. No cab driver had ever let her down.

She would spend the afternoon walking in one of the parks and in the evening she would go out alone to a small bar she had found on her second visit, where she could enjoy a meal and bottle of wine without interruption.

The following morning her alarm would wake her at 5.00 and the taxi would arrive at 5.30 to take her back to the airport where she would catch the weekly Saturday flight south to the Falkland Islands.

All that morning they would fly along the Chilean cost, putting down briefly at Puerto Montt and Punta Arenas and even sometimes at Rio Gallegos in southern Argentina. For the last part of the journey, out across the South Atlantic to Mount Pleasant, the military and international civilian airport on East Falkland, some of the seats in the plane would be removed and the space filled with cargo.

At Mount Pleasant she would take the airport bus across 50 miles or so of rough road to Stanley. The bus dropped her near the tourist office and she did the last part of her journey on foot, carrying her suitcase along the seafront to the Malvina House

Hotel. She checked in, confirmed her booking for a Land Rover and driver for Monday, then went up to her room, took off her shoes and lay on the bed relaxing. Apart from basic courtesies she hadn't spoken to another person for 48 hours. She was 8000 miles from her home on Bodmin Moor but felt a great sense of peace, as she did every year on arrival.

As always at this moment she thought back to that dreadful day in late May 1983 when she had learned that Jonathan had been killed at Goose Green. Ralph always maintained he had tried to ring her but couldn't get through. Instead, she had learned the news from someone at work who had seen the name in the paper.

"Jonathan Mounsey – wasn't that your lad? I see he's been killed in the Falklands. I'm so sorry."

The shock was so great that she had gone white and the woman was quite concerned.

"Oh, I'm so sorry. I thought you must have known. Surely they let the parents know first before printing it in the papers."

Yes, of course they let the parents know first. Except she wasn't his mother, even though she still used his father's name. With all the illumination of hindsight, moving in with Ralph Mounsey had been a big mistake. When they first met and began seeing each other he'd seemed a warm, caring man. It was only later she realised that with a deeply-loved wife dead in a car crash and a 9 year old son to bring up on his own, what he really wanted was a surrogate mother, a housekeeper and regular access to sex. Any love he was capable of was still linked to the woman who had died under the wheels of a lorry on the M6.

Her first reaction on making this discovery was to cut her losses and move on but she found she could not leave the boy. He missed his mother so desperately and got no response from his father locked in his own misery, so he turned to her. She had never had a child, never wanted one, but found herself responding to this silent but powerful despair in a way that surprised her. As the years passed and Ralph grew more distant, she and Jonathan became very close until it was hard to remember he was not actually her son.

She rejoiced in the trust he showed her, helped him with his homework like any other mother, and even when they had the occasional spat – as was inevitable during his teenage years – the bond between them was never broken. Jonathan remembered her birthday and always bought her a present on Mother's Day which gave her a shivery feeling up her spine. The day he left school and joined the army was a heart-wrenching moment, one that she had never believed would happen to her.

With Jonathan gone, life with Ralph closed in till there was nothing but sleep, eat and work. Ralph was never unkind, just distant, any spark that was once between them long since extinguished. It was almost, she thought once, as though now that the child had grown up and gone, there was no more need for the surrogate mother either, but he did not know how to get rid of her.

She solved the problem for him by simply packing a case one day and leaving. She rented a tiny flat above a greengrocer's shop and began to think what to do with the rest of her life. She dreaded telling Jonathan what she had done but when she finally summoned up the courage he took it in his stride.

"Good for you, Mum ..." Even after all these years it still gave her a thrill to hear him call her that ... "Don't know why you didn't leave him years ago. He never really needed either of us, did he?"

"He's always taken care of us, Jonathan. He's not an unkind man."

"No, but it was always a bit third-person, wasn't it? Looking after us in the same way as he would a new car, giving it a wash on a Sunday morning and so on."

She had never thought of herself as a new car but she knew what he meant. No unkindness, only distance, locked for ever in self-destructive mourning.

"So what you going to do with yourself now, Mum?"

"I don't really know. I haven't thought."

"Do you need any money. I mean, I haven't got a lot but …"

She was touched by the offer. "No, I'm fine for money. Your Dad's not mean and I've got that little legacy from my father that I've never touched."

"Good for you. Then why not make a complete break. Get away from here. Do something different. Change your life."

She smiled a little at the simplicity of the 20-year-old view but thought little more about it. She settled into a new routine – one where she had more freedom to do what she wanted, make her own decisions, stay up late or get up early, no-one to please but herself.

She saw Jonathan from time to time when he came home on leave and he wrote fairly regularly. They stayed close, or as close as any child will stay to a parent when he is beginning to make his own way in the world.

And then came April 1983 and the Argentinian invasion of The Falklands. At first it meant very little to her. Another conflict, more bad news, something unpleasant happened somewhere every day. But then came the news of the Task Force and the late-night phone call from Jonathan, guarded but explicit.

"I'm going away for a bit, Mum. Can't say where and don't know how long for. Take care of yourself."

"I'll be fine," she said, "Have you told your father?"

"No, haven't had time. You let him know for me, yeah? Give you a call when I get back. Love you." And he was gone.

"Take care of yourself," she said into an empty phone.

But he hadn't taken care of himself, or perhaps that morning at Goose Green for a professional solider with a job to do, taking care of yourself was not an option.

After Jonathan's death, her horizons, already narrow, closed in still further. The tenuous contact that had remained between her and Ralph now came to a complete end. Jonathan had been the last link between them. Now there was nothing.

Once the conflict was over and the self-satisfied flag waving had died down, she began to think again about what Jonathan had said to her when she first left Ralph.

"Why not make a complete break, Mum? Get away from here. Do something different. Change your life."

As the weeks passed and the numbness became more bearable she began to think seriously about what he had said. She had always enjoyed what she did but as a graphic designer she could work anywhere, perhaps even start up on her own. Without really acknowledging to herself that she was doing it, she began to consider where she might like to live and how she might earn a living. Almost imperceptibly the dream blended into reality and in the spring of the following year she bought the little cottage on the edge of Bodmin Moor.

Her final contact with Ralph was in late summer the year before she moved. Mrs Thatcher had announced that, if requested by next-of-kin, the British government would repatriate the bodies of dead British servicemen buried in the Falklands for reburial in Britain. She got in touch with Ralph.

"Will you be asking for Jonathan to be brought home?" she asked him on the phone.

"No. What's the point? The boy's dead. It doesn't matter where he's dead. He's just dead. Like his mother. That's all." And he had hung up.

"Oh, yes, he's dead," she thought, "but he's been dead to you for a long time. He's only recently dead to me and I want to mourn him."

It was then that she conceived the idea. If Ralph – as the only real parent – would not ask for Jonathan to come back to her, then she would go to Jonathan. The thought of the long journey did not worry her.

She felt that she could not rest until she could see where he had died, stood beside his grave and said a proper goodbye.

Calmly and logically, she began to think through what she would have to do and she soon realised that simply going to the place where he died would not be enough. She needed to understand why he had gone, why any of them had gone, what had been achieved beyond the salvaging of national pride.

With some difficulty, hampered all the time by not being a genuine blood relative, she managed to contact his regiment and eventually one of his fellow soldiers. In the end she lied and said she was Jonathan's mother and a meeting was arranged in London.

The young man she met in the bar of the Waldorf Hotel in the Aldwych was called Mark Flotman. He was a thin, wiry young man and a man of few words. He shook her hand, gave her a brief smile and started with a warning.

"I don't know what I can tell you, Mrs Mounsey, but I do know there's a lot I can't tell you."

"I understand. I just wanted to talk to someone who knew Jonathan. Who was with him when … when he died."

"I was with him. We were all there." He paused. "It was a difficult day."

"I don't want details, I'm sure you can't give them anyway. I want … Well, I suppose I want to know if it was all worth it. All those lives."

He gave a short, sharp laugh, almost a bark. "Worth it? No idea, you'll have to ask the historians that. It was successful, that's all I know. We achieved what we were sent to do."

She was silent and he went on more gently. "It's what we trained for, this kind of thing. There's always a risk, some will come through, some will be injured and some …"

"Will die." She finished the sentence for him.

"Yes, but more of them died than we did, poor sods."

Her curiosity was roused. "Why do you say that?"

"Because they were poor sods. Many of their soldiers were just kids. They didn't want to be there any more than we did. They were very young but they fought bravely, even though they weren't very well trained and most of their equipment was crap." He paused for a moment, then added thoughtfully, "Apart from their boots. They had great boots. Much better than ours."

It took longer than she had expected to arrange her first visit to the Falklands and it was not until March 1986 that she finally found herself in Stanley. There were no commercial flights in those days, the only way to get there by air was with the RAF flying from Brize Norton via Ascension Island. The flight was long, but straightforward. It was only later that she realised how lucky she was. Civilian passengers were low in the pecking order and always liable to be bumped if a military need cropped up at the last minute.

Everything was so strange on that first visit. The very appearance of the town of Stanley, so British in many ways. The Victorian villas along the seafront looking like the edge of any provincial town in Britain until you noticed the corrugated iron roofs. It was all somehow out of focus.

She still felt very self-conscious in those days, very aware that many people wouldn't understand why she had travelled so far to see the grave of someone who wasn't her son. She confided in no-one, merely asking at the hotel reception how she could visit Goose Green. There were a number of Falkland Islanders who were available to drive tourists where they wanted to go, so there was no trouble finding a driver with a Land Rover for her.

It was a long journey across a bleak – yet beautiful – landscape, over roads which at times were no more than a track. Firmly, but courteously, she resisted the driver's attempts to talk to her but when they arrived at Goose Green he asked her where she wanted to go.

"To the military cemetery, please", she said.

He seemed surprised. "The Argentine cemetery?" he asked.

She was surprised in her turn. "No, the British cemetery."

"But that's not here. That's at San Carlos. It's the Argentinians who are buried here."

"Oh. But he … that is, my son … was killed here."

The man was sympathetic. "I'm sorry to hear that but he won't be buried here. He'll be at San Carlos. If only you'd said. I could have taken you there but we'd've had to leave a lot earlier. It's a long way."

She sat for a moment looking out across the remote settlement to the sea beyond. Jonathan might not be buried here, but this was where he and Mark and all the others had come ashore. Somewhere round here they had fought, some came through, some were wounded, some had died. It all seemed very peaceful. Death seemed very far away.

The driver was gentle with her. "I'm sorry you've come here without realising," he said. "We don't really have time to go to San Carlos and still get back to Stanley tonight. Why don't I drive you back and I'll take you to San Carlos tomorrow or the next day."

Yes, that made sense. She had travelled 8000 miles to see Jonathan again. Another day wouldn't make any difference.

She turned to the driver to thank him and accept his suggestion but then suddenly she had a flash of memory. Mark Flotman sitting in the bar at the Waldorf saying: "More of them died than we did, poor sods. Many of their soldiers were just kids. They didn't want to be there any more than we did."

Acting on an impulse she found herself saying. "Thank you, I would like that, but you say there is an Argentine cemetery here. Could we just visit that first?"

The man shrugged. "Sure, if you really want to."

She stood alone on the bleak hillside. The driver, while remaining courteous, did not come with her as she climbed the short slope to the cemetery enclosed in a low stone wall. Inside she looked at the rows of white crosses, all someone's sons who never came home. After a while she noticed that many of the crosses had no names on them, anonymous dead in a conflict desired only by military leaders and politicians.

Curiously she felt very close to Jonathan here and it was nearly half an hour before, sensing the growing impatience of her driver, she walked back down the path to the Land Rover.

Bouncing back along the track she asked him about the nameless crosses.

"Many of their soldiers didn't have any identification on them. No names, no identities. No reason for them not to have a grave though."

"But what about the families? Don't they want to see where their sons are buried?"

He shrugged. "Most of them don't come here. Only a few. Only direct family members are allowed in anyway, but I guess most people simply can't afford it."

"Only direct family?"

"That's right, and they have to come in organised groups. You must realise there's not a lot of love for the Argentinians in these islands. As far as we're concerned, we were invaded by a foreign power."

"But these were just boys."

"Boys with guns who attacked us. Oh, don't get me wrong. I have a proper respect for the dead. But that doesn't mean I have to welcome crowds of Argentinians with open arms."

She was silent. She felt anything she said would be inadequate. She had never been invaded, never had a loaded gun pointed at her, never faced military occupation of her home. How could she make a judgement? And yet, running through her mind was the thought that if the position had been reversed and the same rules applied, she would not have been allowed to come here and say goodbye to Jonathan.

She was not 'direct family'.

Two days later she went to San Carlos and stood beside Jonathan's grave. She laid no flowers, she could imagine his wry smile if he saw her do that, but she stood for several minutes thinking about her son who was not her son, the young boy who had clung to her desperately in his loneliness and despair. The young boy who had grown to be a man and still called her Mum. This is where it came to an end.

"Goodbye, Jonathan," she said softly and as she turned away the wind, which was never still on East Falkland, ruffled her hair lightly as though a hand had been passed over it. She walked back to the Land Rover knowing that she would not visit this grave again. She had done what she had come to do. She had laid Jonathan to rest in her mind.

She had a few more days before the RAF would transport her back to the UK. She spent the next day walking restlessly around Stanley. An idea was growing in her mind but she was not entirely comfortable with it and wanted to examine it from all sides. By the end of the day she was still uncomfortable but equally sure it had to be done. That night in the hotel she asked them to find her another driver, another Land Rover, and the following day she went back to Goose Green, to the little cemetery with so many unnamed crosses.

This time she took with her a small posy of white flowers. She chose an unknown grave at random and stood before it for a moment.

"I've come to say goodbye," she said softly into the wind and bending, she laid the small posy at the foot of the cross. "Whoever you are, from your mother wherever she is, I hope you rest in peace."

She stood there for some while, her thoughts ranging from Jonathan, to the futility of war, to her own solitude, to the many mothers in Argentina who, like her, grieved for those they had lost but who, unlike her, would never achieve that final closure. She stood in absolute silence except for the sighing of the wind and the distant murmur of the sea.

At length she took one last look at the little white cross in front of her and the small bunch of flowers she had laid there and turned away, back to the Land Rover, back to the RAF, back to England and the cottage on the edge of Bodmin Moor.

Her driver looked at her strangely as she climbed back into the Rover.

"What did you do that for?" he asked.

"Because his mother can't," she answered.

The following year she made the same journey, and this time laid her offering at a different cross, and the year after she came again. Eventually, when commercial flights via Santiago began, her journey became easier and she fell into the rhythm of coming every May – the month Jonathan had died – to fulfil what she had come to believe was a pilgrimage, to do for those unknown boys something which their own mothers could not do.

In the village on the edge of Bodmin Moor they think she is eccentric. In Stanley, although they now know her well – they think she is slightly crazy. But as far as she is concerned it is all perfectly normal.

And she is at peace with herself.

THAT'S A FUNNY LOOKING CLOUD

The Isle of Avalon

Sitting here. Looking out. Garden. Grass. Flowers. What are they? I'm sure I know but I can't think. Red. Beautiful scent. I can smell them when the window's open. Looks like thorns on their stems. Red. R ... I know what they are. I know I know. It's on the tip of my tongue ... No, it's gone.

Sky. Blue. Oh, that's a funny looking cloud. Looks like a car. A white car in the sky. Moving quite fast. Where's my car? If I had my car I could go home. I would like to go home.

There's that woman again. I'm sure she's wearing my dressing gown. But if she is, whose dressing gown am I wearing?

Here comes that bustley lady. What is it this time? Tea? "Oh, yes, please. Thank you."

I don't know what this place is but they're obsessed by tea. Every time I empty one cup, another one arrives in its place. If I was back home I'd only have tea when I wanted it, not just because someone brings it.

I'm sure that's my dressing gown. This one doesn't feel right. If I was at home I could check in the wardrobe. I don't know how to check on things like that here.

When am I going home? No-one ever seems able to tell me. "Oh, excuse me … I'm waiting for my car so I can go home. Can you tell me when it's coming?"

No, she's gone, but at least she smiled. They don't all smile.

Sky. Oh, that's a funny looking cloud. Bit like a car. I can't remember what I did with my car.

The first car I ever drove was Dad's Wolsey 25 just before the war. I was too young to drive really but he let me take it round the paddock, and then one weekend when Mother was away he let me drive him into the village. Naughty but nice. By the end of the war I was driving staff cars. Smart uniform. Peaked hats. Stiff brim. Haven't seen that hat lately. Wonder where I put it? Perhaps she's taken it. Wears it with my dressing gown.

I wonder why Dad doesn't come and see me anymore.

Those flowers are nice. Red. Lovely scent when the window's open. Not sure what they are? Think I've seen them before.

I don't really want this tea. If I have much more tea I'll have to go and spend a penny and then someone will sit in my chair. You can't be too careful round here. They're a funny lot, you know. That woman over there, for instance, in that blue and white dressing gown. I had a dressing gown like that once.

It'll be dinner time soon. Chicken, I suppose. It's always chicken. I like chicken but it would be nice to have a change sometimes.

Oh, there's that man again. I see him here quite often. Sometimes he has a little girl with him. Yes, there she is. He's nice. She's sweet. He smiles at me and holds my hand so I smile back. I like people who smile.

The only thing is he talks to me and seems to expect an answer. I never know what to say. I don't really know what he's talking about so I just smile. Sometimes I pat his hand to show him I'm listening.

My granddad pats my hand. We sit at the table in the garden of his cottage in Ash. Tea in my own little cup, smaller than theirs. Granny's homemade scones with her own jam, batting the wasps away and laughing, always laughing. Granddad pats my hand and gives me a penny before I go home.

And now I'm patting this man's hand. I show him the funny looking cloud. Try and explain how it looks like my car but that seems to make him sad. His mouth is still smiling but I can see sadness in his eyes.

I pat his hand again to show I'm sorry for whatever it is making him sad, and he calls me "Mum". Why would he do that? It isn't my name. My name is Joan.

I wish I knew what this place was and why that woman is wearing my dressing gown. Whose dressing gown am I wearing? That's the question.

We don't bother about dressing gowns in the Blitz. When the siren goes we just grab whatever is handy, coat, jacket, blanket, and go and sit under the stairs. We don't seem to get the raids here. Haven't heard the sirens lately.

Perhaps that's it. Perhaps we've all been evacuated. Somewhere out in the country where the bombs don't reach. I like the quiet but I wish I knew what had happened to my car. If I had my car I could go home. Dad will be getting anxious if I'm away much longer. I don't know why he hasn't come to get me. It's a worry.

That old lady over there, the one in the blue and white dressing gown, she talks to herself sometimes. Walks up and down all the time like a parrot in a cage. It must be awful to get old like that.

Oh, look, that's a funny looking cloud. Moving ever so fast. I like clouds. They look a bit like white mountains moving across the sky … Except that one – that one reminds me of a car.

They tried to make me have a bath standing up

this morning. Silly idea. Water coming out of the ceiling, splashing everywhere. I wasn't having that. You need to lie down in a bath. Relax. You can't relax standing up. I don't like to be difficult. They're very nice really but I wasn't having that. We had quite struggle. We all got very wet. Can't see the point.

The man is talking again. He looks anxious. Give him another smile. Dad always tells us to smile at people. "A smile is as good as a gift," he says. "You can light up someone's day just by giving them a smile."

I don't think I'm lighting up this man's day. He's still smiling but I don't think he's happy. Now he's talking about grandchildren. This is a puzzle. He doesn't look old enough to have grandchildren. The little girl with him can't be his grandchild. She's not young enough or he's not old enough. Whichever it is.

Some of the people here say they've got grandchildren. Doesn't seem very likely. It's the young ones that have been evacuated, not the grandparents. I think they must be confused.

That man over there, the one in the brown cardigan, I think he's definitely confused. He mutters to himself a lot and sometimes gets angry. He shouts at us. "You lot, you're all away with the fairies," he says. That's silly. There's no such thing as fairies so how can we be away with them? When he starts his shouting, I turn away and find something nice to look at.

Oh, there are those lovely flowers in the garden again. The red ones. I point them out to the nice man, the one with the little girl. He nods. "Roses", he says. That's it. Roses. I knew that. They have a beautiful scent. You can smell them when the window's open.

Dad doesn't have time for gardening but Grandma's garden is always a wealth of colour. The red things ... roses, that's it ... and yellow flowers, blue and white ones, pink. It all looks so lovely.

Granddad doesn't really care much for flowers. "Flowers are for women," he says, "give me a good cauliflower, nice firm cabbage, rows of carrots. That's what you want on your Sunday dinner plate."

Oh, dear, I think the little girl is crying. Where's my handkerchief? That's it. Come here, dear, let me wipe those tears. There's nothing to be sad about.

Oh, that was a big hug, wasn't it. She is a friendly little thing. On my lap? Well, yes ... I suppose ... Oh, why not? Here, up you come. Now dry those eyes. Look at that funny looking cloud up there. Don't you think it looks a bit like a car?

See that lady over there, dear, the one in the blue and white dressing gown? Isn't that a pretty colour. I've got a blue and white frock at home that's ever so pretty. I wore it when Dad and Mother took me to a dinner dance. We went in a hired car. With a chauffeur. I felt like a princess. I love dancing, don't you. I danced all evening. My feet really ached at the end of it. In fact they still ache a bit. But it was worth it. We had a grand night. Perhaps that's why I feel a bit tired this morning.

I don't remember going home. I must have been so tired. I don't remember what I've done with my car either. Perhaps it's in the garage for servicing. Perhaps they'll bring it back tomorrow and then I can go home.

It will be dinner time soon. Fish pie. It's always fish pie. I quite like fish pie but it would be nice to have a change sometimes. Perhaps Granddad will bring me some of his carrots when he comes.

This little girl on my lap's getting a bit heavy but I don't like to move her. The weight on my knees reminds me of something. Oh, what is it? I seem to have trouble remembering things lately. Very frustrating.

Here comes the bustley lady again. What is it this time? Oh, pills. I don't really need pills but she looks so sad if I say no. It's easier to take them. I don't like people looking sad. She makes the little girl get down, gives me a glass of water. I don't want water. I don't want these pills but they never listen.

I try and tell her I don't want them but it's no

good. The man seems to want me to take them too, though what it's got to do with him, I don't know. Ah, well, anything for a quiet life. Where's the glass, pill, sip swallow. Pill, sip swallow. Pill, sip, swallow. There. Everyone happy now?

Oh, look, that's a funny looking cloud. Looks a bit like a car. I drive Dad's car when I go home. He's sold the Wolsey, got an Alvis now. A Grey Lady – beautiful name for a beautiful car. I keep looking out for one when we watch television so I can show people what a beautiful car I drive but I never see one in any of the programmes. None of the cars on the television are beautiful. It's very sad.

I try and tell the man and the little girl about the Alvis but I don't think they understand.

The little girl. She's very sweet. Wonder what she's doing here? Ah, now I remember. The weight on my knees. It was a cat. At least, I think it was. Can't remember its name but I have this vague memory of it sitting on me and purring. It puts a paw on my arm to stop me knitting as the movement of the needles disturbs it. It is funny. Yes, I am sure it was a cat. I wonder where it is. I hope it's all right. I hope someone is feeding it properly.

It will be dinner time soon. Another stew I suppose. It's always stew. I don't mind stew but it would be nice to have a change sometimes. Perhaps they'll put a bit in a bag for me that I can take home to the cat.

I am sure it was a cat on my lap. I can remember it … I think. At least I think I can. I seem to have trouble separating memory from dreams these days. It's all very confusing. No, I am sure there was a cat. She catches water rats along the river and leaves them in the kitchen. Mother always gets very cross when she does that and Dad has to move them but they're only really cat presents, aren't they. Presents to show she loves us.

It's good to be loved …

It's good to have someone to love …

I'm sure I had someone to love once … Lots of someones … I don't know where they are now …

I don't know what this place is. They're all very kind but I do feel terribly lonely sometimes …

Oh, the man's going, and the little girl. Oh, don't start crying again, dear. I'm sure it will all be all right in the long run, whatever it is. This always seems to be a difficult moment for him, for both of them. I'm not sure why.

"Goodbye Mum," he says. I try and tell him my name's Joan but he doesn't seem to understand. Never mind. He'll probably be here again tomorrow. Or the next day. Perhaps he works here. No, that can't be right. They wouldn't let him sit beside me for so long if he worked here, would they? And what about the little girl? She certainly doesn't work here, does she.

Oh, well, I don't know. He's very nice, whoever he is, and so is she. I'm glad they come. He smiles at me and I smile back and pat his hand. See you tomorrow, dear, or the day after that or the day after that. I'll be here.

Unless Dad comes to take me home.

Alone again. Though I'm always alone really. Even when people are talking to me I feel alone. I don't seem to ... don't know ... connect any more. Sometimes I feel as though I'm talking to people through a sheet of glass. I can see them. I can sort of hear them but not properly and I don't think they can hear me either.

It's very disconcerting. Sometimes, just sometimes, it's as though a door opens briefly and for a moment everything makes sense. And then the door shuts and it's gone again.

Ah, well, that's life I suppose. At least I have the scent of those... those... those red flowers coming in the window.

It's quite peaceful here really. Oh, look, that's a funny looking cloud. Looks a bit like a car.

Soon be dinner time. Chicken again, I suppose, always chicken.

Perhaps I'll just have a little nap first ...

SAND BETWEEN THE TOES

The Isle of Wight

He burst into tears when his mother told him they would not be spending their summer holidays at Westgate-on-Sea this year.

"But we always go to Westgate."

"Yes, but this year Dad and I thought we'd like a change."

"Well, I don't want a change. I want to go to Westgate. I want to ride on the donkeys. I want to build a sandcastle and not let the sea knock it down. I want to climb the cliffs. I want to play cricket on the beach. I want to …"

He could not imagine any summer holiday except Westgate. They had been going there for the last five years, ever since he was six. He knew from looking in the photograph albums that there had been other holidays before that – Uncle Ted's bungalow at Pevensey Bay and when Grandpa was alive they would go to his cottage at Sandwich – but he could not actually remember any of them. Westgate was what he remembered and Westgate was what he wanted.

"Dad and I have booked us a place in Sandown."

Sandown. Sandown. How could Sandown compete with Westgate? He did not even know where Sandown was.

"It's on the Isle of Wight."

"I want to go to Westgate.

Gradually as the weeks passed he began to get used to the idea. He knew, with the brutal knowledge of childhood, that once his parents had made up their minds there was nothing he could do about it. Adults decided what would happen and children just had to do it. That was the way of the world.

"When I'm grown up," he said to himself, "I'll take my children to Westgate every year."

This summer of 1957 was going to be significant in more than one way. This was the year he would finish at his primary school and, after the summer holidays, he'd be going to big school, grammar school, French, Latin, learning to play rugger and ... homework.

He was not sure he welcomed the change though he knew it was inevitable. Part of him was excited, but another part wanted to cling on to the familiar and all of him still wanted to go to Westgate.

However, as the time for the holiday drew nearer, he felt the familiar old excitement taking hold. He was still sad about Westgate but the thrill of that oh, too short summer holiday was the sea. He did not know anything about the Isle of Wight but he knew that "isle" was another word for "island" and islands were surrounded by sea.

Living as they did in a south London suburb in a small terrace house, identical to every other terrace house in the street and the next street and the street after that, the annual fortnight by the sea was a beacon on a hilltop, a glimmer of sun through the clouds, a dream that you knew – with patience – would come true.

That fortnight meant freedom, no school, no tidying your bedroom, no excessive knee washing. It meant the whole family together all day – even Dad. It meant the excitement of a strange bed in a strange room, unusual meals, buses that were a different colour. It meant ice creams, strange fizzy drinks, a bucket and spade, a chance to sail your model yacht (even though it usually capsized the moment the wind blew), walks along cliff tops, games of cricket, donkey rides, sand in your clothes and above all the never ending swish and slurp of the living, rising, falling sea.

When he discovered that their guest house – or private hotel, as Dad called it – was on the seafront and that Dad had managed to secure a family room with a view over the sea, he began to think that Sandown might rival Westgate after all. He wondered what the Isle of Wight would be like. In his atlas it looked quite small so you could probably walk all round it in a day, he thought. He quite liked that idea. To set off in the morning in one direction and arrive back in the evening at the place where you started but coming from a different direction. He made the mistake of mentioning this plan to his grandmother, who fortunately was not coming with them as all she ever wanted to do was to sit in a corner and knit something.

"Don't be silly," she said, "you could never walk that far in a day."

"You couldn't," he thought, "but I bet I can".

He began to think about the journey. If they were going to an island they would have to go by ship somehow. For one wild moment he imagined that they would have a raft that Dad would have made, like the Kon-Tiki raft they had learned about in school. He thought of how he would help Dad load all their luggage onto the raft and then Dad would push it off from the shore and steer their way across to the Isle of Wight using a long pole. Mum would sit in the middle holding the twins, who were too young to be allowed loose on a raft, but he would be up the front, keeping his eyes open and warning Dad of any obstacles.

It was a lovely idea but he was eleven now. In a few months' time he'd be learning algebra so he knew that sailing on a raft was only a fantasy.

However, the reality when it eventually came was nearly as exciting. The journey was in many parts, a bus to their nearest station, a local train to Waterloo and then on to the express train for Portsmouth. He had a window seat and watched, entranced, as the city slipped away to be replaced first by scattered houses in open spaces and then by fields and woods. When the train stopped at Portsmouth Town he expected they would get out but, no, apparently, their train went right onto the harbour.

Out of their carriage, shuffling along with all the other people, and then onto to a sort of sloping grid. He could see their ship moored against the harbour wall and on the last stage of the grid, looking down, he could see the sea underneath his feet. Once they were on the boat they went up on deck and for the first time he experienced the excitement of watching the land slip gently away behind them as the ship chugged its way out into the Solent.

A strange feeling came over him then and somewhere, deep inside, he sensed that this was only the first voyage he would take, watching a coastline fade behind him as he began a new journey. He did not understand the feeling, it was like an ache inside him, but a nice ache, almost as though he were coming home. This was a new experience, this was different. Perhaps if he could handle this, he could handle grammar school as well.

This particular journey was a short one and it was not long before they reached the pier at Ryde and were queuing again to get off the boat. Another train ride – much shorter this time – then a walk through the town with Dad carrying the suitcases and they were there. The Culver Private Hotel and a front bedroom with their big trunk sitting in the middle of the floor waiting for them. He rushed across to the bay window and, yes, there was the road and beyond the road the beach and beyond the beach the sea. He gave a deep sigh and Westgate slipped a little further into memory. This was their home for the next two weeks. He could sit in this room, with all his things around him, and he could see the sea.

Later that afternoon before tea they played cricket on the beach. There were little hard wrinkles of sand that he could feel, even through his plimsolls, but if he took them off the sand tickled the soles of his feet and got between his toes so they felt all scratchy when he put his socks back on. The little hard wrinkles of sand caused the ball to bounce off in any direction, making it hard to hit for the person batting. He loved family cricket with Dad's own cricket rules –

you couldn't be out first ball and the LBW law was ignored completely. When fielding he liked being behind the wicket, but nothing could compare with the joy of batting, the smack of the bat against the tennis ball and sometimes the additional joy of seeing it plop into the sea.

The Culver Private Hotel laid on a special tea for young children so at half past five they made their way back there for the twins to have their meal. But not him. Another excitement. Earlier in the day Mum had said to him:

"Now that you're growing up, Peter, Dad and I thought you ought to stay up and have dinner with us in the evenings after the twins have gone to bed."

"Now that you're growing up." That phrase hummed in his mind. 'Growing up' meant a lot of changes. He stiffened his shoulders ready for the challenge and pushed the anxiety of Latin and rugger further into the future.

That first evening he learned that soup was quite nice, so long as it was tomato, that grown-ups seemed inordinately fond of wet, steamy vegetables and that coffee was a drink he could well do without. But nothing could detract from the fact that he was wearing a white shirt and his new school blazer and was having grown-up dinner with his parents.

After dinner he fully expected to be told to go to

bed but there was another surprise.

"It's not a good idea to go straight to bed after a big meal," Dad explained, "so why don't you and Mum go for a walk. I'll stay here and listen out for the twins."

His mother saw the look of joyous amazement on his face and smiled. "Come on," she said, "we'll go for a walk along the seafront."

It was like being transported into another world, a grown-up world, an exciting world. One of the best bits was having Mum to himself for once, never easy to achieve in a family of five. But that wasn't the only thing. Sandown in the evening was a different place to Sandown during the day. There was music coming from the pier and people strolling about, some playing the slot machines in the arcades and all the while the scent of hot dogs and chips hung on the air.

And so ended the first day of his holiday. A day which offered a glimpse of future freedoms to come. As he lay in bed before sleep, watching the lights of the passing buses reflected on the ceiling, he could hardly wait for the next day to come, and the day after that and the day after that …

The holiday he had half feared, as it could never be as good as Westgate, continued to expand in ways he could hardly believe. The following morning he woke early and could see the dust fairies, as his little sister called them, dancing in the sun that sneaked through the curtains. He lay as still as he could for a while but he was desperate to get up and something of his restlessness must have penetrated for finally Dad opened one eye and peered at him over the eiderdown.

"You awake, Peter?"

"Yes."

"Well, I'm not. Neither are Mum and the twins. Why don't you get dressed quietly and go out for a walk. Quietly mind."

"On my own?"

"Why not? You're eleven now. Just be careful crossing the road. Okay?"

"Okay."

"Oh, and take your watch and make sure you're back in time for breakfast. Eight o'clock sharp. Now, goodnight."

He pulled on his shirt, shorts and plimsolls, let himself out of the front door and carefully crossed the road to where the seafront and beach awaited him. He stood there for a moment, the sea and sky in front of him, the only person awake in the whole wide world and he was suddenly engulfed by a new sense of freedom.

That first morning he ran right along the seafront as far as the boating lake, way beyond the amusement arcades and then had to run even faster on the way back so as not to be late for breakfast. While he was munching his cornflakes Mum asked him.

"Where did you go? What did you see?" and he found he could not answer her. There had been so much to see, he could remember none of it.

The second morning he moved more slowly, looking at things around him and before many days had passed he was only walking, not going nearly so far, but seeing much more than he ever did by running. One morning he only went a few yards before finding a strange-shaped piece of seaweed on the beach and sat there for nearly half an hour, looking at it, fingering it, wondering what kind of seaweed it was and where it had come from. He pictured it growing in some far off country, being torn away in a high wind, then floating on the sea, carried by the currents until it reached Sandown beach.

He tried to explain about the seaweed to his parents. Dad was mildly interested but Mum seemed to understand what he could not put into words and asked him lots of questions which he stumbled to answer.

These early morning walks gradually became the high spot of his day. After breakfast he was with the family, playing on the beach, going for a walk across the cliffs, taking a coach trip to Alum Bay or

Carisbrooke Castle. He enjoyed all these activities but he found that things were tumbling over themselves – too much to do, too little time.

He loved the visit to Carisbrooke and would have been quite happy sitting on the battlements looking out over the countryside, imagining what it was like to live in a room built of stone, how you would feel if your way of life was threatened by someone against whom the only defence was a strong outer stone wall.

When he mentioned this to Mum she smiled and said, "You didn't just live in a place like this in times of danger. This would be your home. Think about it. Not much light, cold stone, bad enough in the day perhaps, but think how gloomy it would be at night."

He thought for a moment. "Not very comfortable you mean."

"Not really. No carpets, only rough tables and chairs, no heating other than an open fire in the main hall. Doesn't sound very cosy, does it?"

"No-o." He paused, gathering his thoughts. "But then, you wouldn't know what you were missing, would you? I mean, you'd never have had a carpet or an electric fire or anything."

"That's true."

He ran his hand along the rough stone, feeling its texture, its warmth on one side where the sun had stroked it, the cold, almost damp feel on the side that was permanently in shade. He wondered what other hands had touched these stones, who had stood in this spot before him, enjoying the sunset or watching the remorseless approach of an enemy. He would have liked to stay there longer, using his sense of touch to spur his imagination, but he was swept up in the family undertow. They had to see the museum, the drawbridge, the donkey in the wheel pulling water up from the well, things tumbling on top of each other, too much to see, too much to do, knowing they would have to leave as soon as the coach was ready to go.

On his morning walks he could control the time – so long as he was back for breakfast. On the family activities time controlled him.

One afternoon they were making their way back to the Culver Private Hotel from the bus stop up near the railway station. They had walked over the headland that afternoon and down into Bembridge and then caught the bus back to Sandown. It had been a long walk and the twins were tired. Dad was carrying Joan and Mum was holding Richard's hand coaxing the little boy along with the promise of tea. He was some way behind them when suddenly his attention was caught by a strange array of bricks over a doorway. The front door of the house opened straight onto the street and the house itself was built of quite ordinary bricks. However, over the doorway itself bricks of a different colour and shape had been used to create a kind of arch. The doorway did not need an arch so the bricks must have been laid like that for decoration. He paused to look more closely and saw how they had been neatly fitted together, not just to make an arch, but so that the different colours formed a pattern.

"I wonder who decided to do that," he thought. "Was it the person who planned the house? The builder? The person the house was being built for or just a sudden idea by the man who was laying the bricks?"

He stood back a bit to see it in perspective. It was a delightful sight and made the house look completely different from those on either side. He imagined that he was the bricklayer, standing back to admire his work in context, then, as if from a great distance he heard Richard's voice, the voice of his younger brother who was tired and hungry.

"Mum, mum, look, Peter's lingering."

He sighed and turned, expecting to be told to hurry up and come along but to his surprise he saw his mother give Richard's hand to Dad and then she came walking back towards him.

"I'm sorry ..." he began but she shushed him

with a quick smile.

"What have you found?" she asked. He showed her the strange arrangement of bricks and she seemed to understand. Like him she stood back from the wall to get the full effect and then she smiled.

"It's lovely, isn't it? Different. Whoever did that had an eye for beauty."

"It makes the house stand out, Mum. It makes it different from all the rest."

"Indeed it does. How did you spot it?"

He thought about it. He wasn't sure. "I don't know. I just saw it. I like looking at things. Really looking at them. Having time to think about them, not just rushing off to whatever's next."

He paused, feeling rather embarrassed, but his mother just nodded.

"It's a busy old world, isn't it?" she said. "Does us good to linger sometimes."

He struggled to express feelings that he hardly knew he had. "Sometimes I feel ... pushed ... It's like being on my bike going downhill when the brakes aren't working properly."

He looked up at her, half expecting her to laugh but she just nodded thoughtfully. "I know. Things take you over and sometimes it's difficult to stop them." For a moment she seemed lost in thought then she looked down at him and smiled.

"Never stop looking, Peter. You never know what you might find. But you won't see anything unless you look for it."

He thought that was a rather obvious thing to say. Of course you had to look for something if you wanted to find it, but then he thought, "But I didn't want to find the bricks. I didn't know they were there. And I didn't know I would find that seaweed the other day." And he began to get a glimmer of what his mother meant.

"Does everyone see things they're not looking for?" he asked, struggling to express the not fully formed thought in his mind.

His mother laughed, but a nice laugh as though she were laughing with him, not at him.

"No, they don't," she said, "in fact very few people see anything apart from the things they expect to see."

His brow furrowed. Another new thought. It was proving to be a strange afternoon and all because he stopped to look at a few bricks. He looked up at her wondering how he was supposed to react. Not sure what to say in reply. She must have realised this because she smiled again.

"Don't worry about lingering, Peter. It's good to linger sometimes – it can give you time to sort out what you really think. And being curious is how we learn, so it's good to see with your own eyes, and you do a lot of that, don't you?"

Was she talking about the seaweed, he wondered, *or about living in Carisbrooke Castle?*

He must have showed his disquiet because she quickly came to his rescue. "Now look – Dad and I need to get the twins back for tea. They're very tired. But no need for you to rush. You stay here for a bit if you want. You know what time dinner is, just get back in time to have a wash first. All right?"

"All right." He watched her make her way back to the rest of the family and then turned to look at the bricks again. He wasn't quite sure how it had happened, or what had happened exactly, but somehow he knew he'd been granted another freedom. His mother had given him something precious and while he didn't understand exactly what it was, he sensed that he would come to value it in time.

And I did. Fifty-two years have passed since I first spotted those bricks and now I'm standing looking at them again. I was slightly surprised to find them still here, so much else has changed. If my mother thought it was a 'busy old world' in 1957, then I don't know what she would have made of 2010.

We came back to Sandown for one more holiday after that first one and then moved on to other places. By then I was more used to change. The challenge of grammar school had been faced and, although I didn't particularly enjoy it, we reached an accommodation with each other. I learned Latin, I learned French, I learned I didn't like playing rugger, but perhaps the most important lesson I learned was that institutions of whatever kind do not always welcome individuals.

I was lucky, I suppose. My parents always encouraged me to think for myself, make my own decisions. In the innocence of childhood, I thought all parents were like mine until I grew up and discovered they weren't. My mother in particular, did not so much teach me, as allow me the freedom to learn for myself. With hindsight I can see that they wanted to help me become me, not hurry me into a mirror image of themselves. I will always be grateful for that.

To be honest I'm not quite sure why I've come back to Sandown now after all these years. Inevitably, as time passed, the pace of life speeded up. Lingering was not always an option – and like many other people I found I was often running like mad to stay still. But somehow, in a funny sort of way, in the telescoped inaccuracy of memory, I feel that my life, my real life, began here. Perhaps that's it. Now, in this moment of sadness, I'm reaching back to find something stable on which I can begin to rebuild. That may be fanciful, but whatever the reason, here I am.

Sandown today is very different from the place I remember, of course. The Culver Private Hotel has gone, so has the hot dog stall that stood near it on the front. The boating lake has become a crazy golf course. But the sea is still there, and so is the sand with its little hard wrinkles where would-be Joe Roots now swing their bats with the same glee and enthusiasm as I, a would-be Peter May, once hit sixes into the sea. For me the substance of Sandown has not changed.

Which is why I have come back again, seeking solace which I know I may not find. In spite of all the changes that have taken place in the world, and in me, since that summer of 1957, the basic things still remain. The ability to take pleasure from the shape of a leaf, the cadence of a piece of music, a shadow glimpsed on a blind, the smell of the salt sea in the early morning, the feel of old stone under my hand.

And the realisation that my mother was secretly just the same.

That is why I am here, staring at my bricks again and I am pleased to find they still speak to me even after all these years. They were put there, not just out of necessity but from a desire on someone's part to create something attractive. They touched my eleven-year-old soul all those years ago, and they touch me still.

In a while I will walk down to the beach, maybe even take my shoes off and feel the sand ridges under my bare toes. But first I will look at my bricks for a little longer. I will linger here a while and try to learn again the lesson of moving slowly.

THERE'S NOT A LOT OF PUFFINS IN PINNER

Shetland Islands

They sit on the heather side by side as they would sit in a pub or on a London bus. The wind blows. The gulls scream. They gaze.

"There," says Janet, "down there."

"Where?" says John.

"Down there. To the right of that pointed rock. There's definitely one there."

"Well, I can't see it."

"You're not looking. See where that grassy strip meets the rocks?"

"Yes."

"Come out about ten feet and there's an odd-shaped outcrop, like a sheep with a hump. Got it?"

"Yes …"

"Then about twenty yards to the right there's a sharp, pointy rock."

"There's a lot of rocks there."

"Of course there are. That's why I'm describing the right one so precisely. It's sort of white with seaweed stains all over it."

"Yes, I think I see."

"Well, just to the right of it, see, there's one swimming down there."

"I can't see anything."

"Oh, John, I don't think you're trying."

But really she thinks he is trying. Very trying. John Kennedy, resident of Pinner, in the county of Middlesex.

"Well, I don't think there's anything down there at all. And if there was it'd be damned unfair if you saw a puffin and I didn't."

"It's got nothing to do with fairness. You just need to look in the right place."

"Oh, Janet, for heaven's sake."

Janet Kennedy, also resident of Pinner in the county of Middlesex, which for all practical purposes no longer exists except in the minds of the Post Office and the English cricketing authorities.

"I think you're winding me up. There's nothing there."

"Yes, there is. Look, there, swimming round that corner."

John is straining forward, almost falling over the cliff edge in his efforts to spot a puffin. "I can't see anything. Oh, this is so unfair. I'm the one who wanted to see puffins. You don't give a toss."

Janet, bored with the argument, leans back on

her hands. "Not true. I'm interested in the same way I'm interested in giraffes or camels or hammerheaded sharks. I like the idea of seeing them when they're not framed by the television screen, but I wouldn't go out of my way to look for them."

"Well, I would."

Janet sighs. "Yes, which is why we're stuck in here in Shetland instead of relaxing in a threestar hotel with swimming pool in Majorca. Might just as well have stayed at home."

"Not an option. There's not a lot of puffins in Pinner."

Pinner, for those who may not have stumbled across it in their frantic attempts to avoid the traffic jams on the North Circular, is a suburb in northwest London. Surrounded by such places as Watford, Harrow, Ruislip and Rickmansworth, Pinner has very little to distinguish it from dozens of other London suburbs. Nevertheless, it happens to be where Janet and John Kennedy live. In number 14 – which would be number 13 were it not for superstitious builders – Casablanca Avenue.

"Are." There are moments when Janet's love of accuracy overcomes her need for caution.

"Pardon?"

"'*Is*' is not grammatically correct in that sentence."

John has lost the thread of the argument.

"Do what?"

"There *are* not a lot of puffins in Pinner."

"I know. That's why we're here."

"You said 'is' and you should have said 'are'. Puffins are plural."

"They're not even singular at the moment. I think that was a duck."

"What was?"

"What you saw swimming around down there. If you saw anything at all."

Both Janet and John are capable of going on like this for some time – conversation taken straight out of the 1950s reading books after which they were doubtless both named. A mechanical conversation, in which each know their lines and deliver them without feeling, anticipating the answer before it comes.

"I still don't understand this sudden passion for puffins. It's not some sort of corporate initiative test, is it?"

"Of course not. And don't keep implying that you're indulging me in some way. You agreed to come here too."

"Well, you'd stand more chance of seeing any puffins if you'd remembered the binoculars."

"I put them out on the bed."

"Just like you do at home. Then leave them there."

"I was going to give them a clean but then you called so I grabbed the camera and came."

He gazes down the cliff with renewed intensity as though sheer willpower could make binocular lenses superfluous. Janet watches him for a moment then turns away. Their routine snippy conversation ceases and their real conversation, the one that never sees the light of day, continues silently.

Don't know why you bought them. We never use them even at home. It's a constant refrain: 'If it's fine this afternoon we could take the binoculars and drive up to the downs.' Only by the time the afternoon comes you're deep in work at your desk and another day slips away from under us.

John too is struggling with thoughts he cannot express aloud: *Why is the theory so easy but the practice so hard? It always seems so logical on a Friday night – this weekend we really will have a break. Go for a long walk. Find that flight of locks on the Grand Union Canal.*

Then I see you working, and I think I might as well just catch up with a few things and then, bingo, suddenly it's Sunday evening and our small patch of shared freedom has gone.

There is a pause until, as so often, the silence between them becomes uncomfortable so they each, separately, decide to start a new topic. Janet begins.

"Quiet here, isn't it?"

"Apart from the birds."

"I meant no people. Makes a change. I didn't know anywhere could be as lonely as this."

"I like it."

"Yes, so do I in a funny sort of way."

Half unconsciously they move a little closer together. John breathes deeply gazing out to sea, a man facing the elements, enjoying the fantasy that he controls his own destiny. Janet trails her hand across the turf, noticing for the first time its roughness and deep green colour. So different from the browning moss and daisy-punctuated square that passes for grass back in Pinner.

Below them a great skua spirals upwards in the wind and hangs for a moment before plunging away again towards the surf. Janet watches it go.

"Did you see that?"

"Yes, I didn't know gulls could hover like that."

"It wasn't really hovering. I think it was just using the wind." She pauses for a moment, brow furrowed. "Was it a gull?"

"Don't know. Must have been. What else is that size?"

"We really ought to get a book. Look it up."

"Yes." A brief pause. "We always say that. We never do."

"Then let's do it tomorrow. There's bound to be a bookshop in Lerwick."

"It's back – look at the way it sort of rides on the wind. It's beautiful."

And for a moment – a brief moment – their thoughts are almost united as they watch the skua – which isn't a gull – as it loops and spirals, does U-turns in the sky and thinks about what skuas mostly think about: where its next meal is coming from.

"What do you suppose Mrs Rae will give us for dinner tonight?"

John shakes his head. "Fish probably, it's been fish of some kind every night so far."

"Main industry of the islands."

"I think that's oil these days."

"Still important to them."

"Hmm. Nice pork chop wouldn't go amiss."

"You chose to come here. We could be in Majorca."

But Janet's response is automatic. A Pavlovian reaction continuing a dialogue that has been running more or less continuously since John first suggested a holiday on Shetland.

"It's not just the puffins. Somewhere quiet, we said. Give us time to talk. Sort out what we're going to do."

"But we're not talking, are we?"

"Yes, we are."

"Not talk talking. We haven't made any decisions."

"It's not that easy."

"Of course it's not that easy. If it were easy, we could have done it over a drink in the Cat and Fiddle and had a normal holiday like everyone else."

"Perhaps that's the problem."

"What?"

"That we want to be like everyone else."

"Everyone else isn't sitting on a deserted cliff top looking at puffins."

"Nor are we."

"Yes we are. Look, there's another one. That's two of them on that rock."

"I can't see them."

"You don't want to see them."

"Yes, I do. This trip was my idea. I've never seen a puffin. Not even in a zoo. And I want to."

"Why?"

"Because they're different and it's something not many people do."

"Yes, they do. Bird watchers come from all over."

"I meant people we know. It's something unusual. It's interesting."

"One of them's just dived into the water. Is that interesting?"

In his agitation John jumps to his feet.

"Where?"

He peers anxiously down the cliff face then slowly sinks back onto the heather.

"I think you're making this up."

"You can't see them because I saw them first, that's all."

"Don't be stupid. I can't see them because you left the binoculars behind."

"They're your binoculars so how can I have left them behind?"

"You're always in such a hurry."

"You always take so long over everything."

"It shouldn't matter. We're on holiday."

"We had a ferry to catch. We had a place booked."

And once again the conversation turns into a loop which curls back on itself in a kind of vocal perpetual motion, round and round, backwards and forwards, getting nowhere – it's only purpose to fill the void and prevent the dangerous silence from intruding. The silence that might force shared thoughts into the open.

Neither of them take offence at the comments of the other. Indeed, they probably barely hear them in the same way as they might walk through a familiar house without noticing the colour of the carpet or the pictures on the walls.

"We wanted somewhere quiet, somewhere away

from it all."

"Well, we got that bit right."

"We never get a chance to talk properly at home."

"You're never in."

"You're always doing something else even when I am."

A pause. Again they sense they're approaching dangerous territory, ideas which are not yet ready for the light of day. Janet picks some grass off her skirt.

It's funny how we always say it'd be nice to have more free time. But when I get free time at home I don't know what to do with it.

Unknowingly John's thoughts are running on similar lines. *When I'm at work or if I'm away I always think longingly of home and wish I were back there. The moment I get there, I don't know what to do.*

I didn't always have this problem with free time. School holidays seemed to be over before they'd really begun. And in term time you longed for the weekend, but blink and you missed it.

The silence hangs heavily between them as, side by side, they gaze out to sea. Then John decides to grasp the nettle. "If you give up work you'll have plenty of time on your hands."

"It wouldn't be giving up work. I'd be working from home."

"Still giving up a salary for the uncertain possibility

of earning freelance fees."

"For which I'll probably have to work harder than I do now. But it will be on my terms."

"Why take the risk?"

Janet pauses to consider her response. She goes to speak, then changes her mind.

It's not a risk, it's a challenge. I want to be in control again. There's so little of our lives we're allowed to control these days. I want to be free to earn a living the way I want to. To succeed because of my own efforts …

For John, too, there are boundaries he isn't yet willing to cross. *It's a gesture. It must be. She's always loved her job. Management suits her. This consultancy thing is just a fad.*

Janet is still absorbed in her own thoughts … *and if I fail, then I fail, but whatever happens, I'll have done it.*

Janet shifts a little on the tussocky grass. She lets her body lean backwards, her weight taken on her arms, and looks upward at the sky. John turns his back on the sea and looks down at her.

"You've decided, haven't you?"

"Not finally."

"You said we'd discuss it together. That it'd be a joint decision."

"We can't discuss it. Every time we do, you try and talk me out of it. That's not a discussion."

"It's not that I don't understand. My life's pretty much routine too."

And always will be, whether he stays a Marketing Director, becomes an ageing hippy or goes in for inter-planetary space travel.

"There has to be something more to aim for than this."

"Yes, there does."

"Something other than work. Something more than filling the hours between breakfast and bedtime. Something with a point to it."

"Oh, for heaven's sake, why do we always analyse it? Why don't we just do it?"

"No, I'm serious. What about what we want? Why don't we concentrate on that?"

"Because we don't know the answer to the question."

A moment of truth. Spoken before she realises what she's saying. A comment that cannot be shrugged away once it has seen the light of day. A thought that now has to be faced unless John is prepared to play the game and pretend it hasn't been said.

"No, we don't. Because we've never asked it?" John does not oblige, and now a crisis point has been reached. By accident. One last attempt …

Janet laughs. "Questions, questions. Does the universe have a point? Is there a God? Is there life on other planets? Will we ever own a TV remote control that works first time?"

But, once started, John will not be diverted. "There was a time when we could talk to each other, exchange ideas as well as information. Listen, as well as speak."

But even as he mourns the passing of that time, John is perpetuating the problem. He is talking, but not listening. Perhaps he isn't even talking to Janet but to himself, the himself of twenty years ago.

Something's missing. Somehow, without realising it, I've slipped off at a tangent. I thought I was moving straight ahead but either the goalposts have been moved or ... or I've changed.

Of course it's both, but John hasn't worked that out yet. The goalposts are constantly changing and so is the route towards them. In fact, the only constant is change itself.

It's become a cliché to say the summers were warmer when we were young, so why can I smell the scent of the spring flowers in my mother's garden so clearly? Why can I hear the playground noise of school more easily than I can hear the sounds of our home in Pinner? Why can I see you in the wrap-around skirt and blouse you wore that day on the beach at Mevagissey, and yet without turning my head I could not say what you're wearing today. What has changed?

Janet has rolled over on her tummy and is gazing out to sea. "There's a boat out there. A big one."

"Yes. Did you see that Russian trawler in the harbour yesterday? Seems funny to see them in British ports."

"Seems funny to think of this as a British port. Did you know we're closer to Norway here than we are to London?"

"I don't feel close to anywhere."

"The air is so clear here ..." She breathes deeply. "You can feel it pouring through you, not clogging up the system."

"There you are. I told you it was a duck."

"What?"

"Down there. Swimming near the rocks. Two of them. Ducks."

"That's not what I saw before."

"I bet it was."

"Of course it wasn't. I know a duck when I see one."

In fact, she doesn't. What they're looking at is a pair of red-throated divers out for a short cruise. But does it matter, this naming of things? The divers are not any less divers for being referred to as ducks. It won't affect their hunting for food, their urge to mate, their instinct for survival. As far as all that is concerned, they could be called elephants and their lives would not be changed by one jot or tittle. No, it doesn't matter to the divers, so why should it matter to Janet?

"There's probably umpty different kinds of duck, if only we knew."

"It'd be nice to know the difference. We must get that book."

"Yes." John pauses for a moment. "You can get DVDs now to help you recognise birds."

"What do you do? Cart your laptop around with you on the cliffs?"

"To watch at home. Help identify different characteristics." He looks across at Janet and the next remark is a cross between a statement and a plea. "We could do that. Something to do together."

If it is a plea, she does not respond to it. "Shall we move on? There's nothing left to see here."

"What about the puffins? We came to see the puffins."

"Well, they're not there now."

"I bet they never were."

"Yes, they were. But they've gone. Come on."

She gets to her feet, brushing down her skirt as she does so. John hugs his knees and doesn't move. Janet looks down. He looks so lonely, so defenceless and for a moment her heart reaches out to him.

Oh, John. Do you remember the day you went for

that seat on the board? We were so thrilled. We'd discussed your proposal together, I typed it up, you amended it, I did the corrections and printed it. I came with you to the interview. Stood outside with you on the pavement, checked your tie was straight, gave you a kiss and sent you in to fight for both of us. And you won. The night we heard we bought a bottle of champagne. Asked the neighbours in. Toasted the future. And then you and I treated ourselves in that little French restaurant round the back of the market. Everything looked bright. Everything was going to be different.

Oblivious of her train of thought, John points out over the sea. "Look at those gulls there, the thin ones. They've got sort of swept back wings like a jet fighter."

"And everything was different."

"Sorry?"

"Doesn't matter."

"Where are we going?"

"Doesn't matter. Anywhere. Come on."

Deep inside John an instinct stirs. It never reaches consciousness, but somewhere – stillborn – lies the thought that it does matter, not now, not which moorland path to take, but the direction for the future must not be left to chance. But no sooner is the faint stirring felt than it is gone, and he scrambles to his feet to join Janet who is already several yards away.

"Come on, slowcoach."

And sighing for something he does not understand he goes to join her, turning his back on the sea and the small group of fulmars – which are also not gulls – gliding below him.

"Why is it that when you're in a wide open space like this anything seems possible and yet when you get back home change of any kind seems too much effort?"

"This isn't real, that's why."

"I'd say it was very real indeed. Better than Pinner."

"I know, but it isn't real for us. This isn't our life. It's almost as though … as though … we've stepped into a postcard."

It isn't real because they're on holiday. For two weeks their real world has gone into suspended animation. They have no demands on their time, no responsibilities. They have the space – if they care to use it – to stop and think or just stop. They've stepped out of their own environment, but for them the process of doing nothing is unnatural and that in itself is unsettling.

"Have you noticed how springy the turf is? I bet it'd be comfortable to sleep on."

John, the nascent explorer, man of action, thrusting his way into the unknown, beating paths out of the wild country, eating off the land, tireless in his quest to find … the puffins.

"Let's make for top of this ridge. See what's on the other side."

Janet, as usual, is more prosaic. "Have we got time to go that far? We've got to get back to the car and make the five o'clock ferry."

"No problem. There's plenty of time."

The path winds upwards and they move along it, Janet half a pace ahead. For a while they are silent, each lost in their own thoughts and in John's case in particular, suddenly conscious of a slight shortage of breath.

I suppose I'm getting old. Late forties and I get breathless walking up a hill. Don't get enough exercise, that's the trouble. Soon get fit again if I had a bit more time.

Up ahead of him, striding out, Janet feels the thick grass rasping at her legs.

I could live here. Walk barefoot on the cliffs, smell the sea, get salt in my hair.

She pauses and in spite of the sun, shivers for a moment.

Bet it's hell here in the winter.

The incline gets shallower and suddenly they reach the top of the ridge and are looking over empty moor land stretching out ahead of them. John pauses.

"This can't be right. We're going away from the sea."

Janet also pauses. She looks about her.

"No, this is an island, remember. I think if we walk across this headland we should come to those high cliffs Mrs Rae told us about. The ones where all the seabirds are."

"Do you think there'll be puffins there?"

"Mrs Rae seemed to think so."

"Come on then."

They walk on. Although they are no longer climbing steeply, the path undulates and is very uneven. Once or twice they miss their footing and stumble. There is no-one else in the landscape, no sign of habitation.

An almost primitive feeling wells up inside John. They are alone in the wilderness. The hire car parked at the Visitor Centre two miles away is conveniently forgotten. He is the man, the explorer, it will only be due to his experience and unflinching determination that they will get back alive.

Half unconsciously he quickens his pace and moves ahead of Janet. The man, the provider, the protector.

Then his feeling of being in control is rudely shattered. Out of nowhere it seems, comes a large bird, flying fast and low, taking John by surprise.

My God, it's a vulture. No, it can't be, we don't have vultures here. Is it an eagle? No, it's too small. Well, whatever it is, it's coming for me.

Instinctively he thrusts up his arm and the bird – which is actually an arctic skua – adjusts its wing feathers, increases its altitude by a few inches, brushes the tips of his fingers and is gone.

"Janet, did you see that?"

"Look, out, John. Here comes another one."

Again a big brown bird comes hurtling out of the heather, narrowly misses John's head and spirals upwards again.

"What on earth's going on? It's like something out of that film."

"I think they must be protecting their nests. Look, let's go faster. If we get away from this area, I think they'll leave us alone."

Janet and John begin an undignified trot across the heath land. Four more times they have to stop and raise their arms above their heads to deflect the low flying skuas but at last the path begins to climb again and they're left in peace.

"What on earth were they? They can't have been eagles, surely?"

"Don't think so. They weren't big enough."

"Well, whatever they were, I think we'll find another route back."

They move on, eying every bird within range with a degree of suspicion. As they approach the crest of the headland, John's excitement begins to increase. Like a child who knows he will definitely get that train set for Christmas so long as he doesn't tread on any cracks on the pavement, he dimly has the idea that if he can just see puffins in the wild, then his world will be changed.

"Nearly there."

They breast the final rise and stop, stunned into silence. The sea, invisible until now, is spread out below and ahead of them. A strong wind buffets their faces. Offshore, a rocky pinnacle rises from the sea to match their height, separated from them by a drop of 600 feet. Thousands of sea birds are wheeling over the cliffs, an assortment of harsh cries fills the air.

Janet and John instinctively reach out and take each other's hands.

"This is amazing," says John.

"It feels like we're standing on the edge of the world," says Janet.

"Just look at all those birds. I've never seen anything like it."

"I never knew there were so many different kinds of gull."

Above them, below them and ahead of them the seabirds spiral and call. Gannets and kittiwakes, guillemots and terns, skuas, razorbills, sheerwaters and fulmars. And, perhaps just to satisfy Janet and John's limited ornithological knowledge, herring gulls, black-backed gulls and common gulls which, ironically, are anything but common.

The scale of the scene before them is like a strong drink. Their senses reel.

"John …"

"Yes, Janet?"

"If you …" But she cannot go on. Overcome by the moment she wants to say something significant, something to reflect the flood of emotion that is pouring through her. But the habit of years is too great.

John, too, is caught up in the moment.

If only life could always be like this. A sense of beauty, a sense of wonder. Seeing this puts everything into perspective.

He turns to Janet at the same moment she turns towards him. They smile, a tentative, shy smile that gradually broadens into a grin. In the wind roaring down from the Arctic Circle they share the warmest moment of their day.

Then John is struck by a sudden thought. His face falls. The brief spark vanishes.

"But the puffins … There aren't any puffins."

The moment has not yet died for Janet. Her face

lights up. She laughs.

"No, not a single puffin in sight."

John is distraught. "But I wanted to see puffins. There's every bird you can imagine here. Why aren't there any puffins?"

"Perhaps they've gone on their summer holidays." Janet is openly laughing now. "Or perhaps they're still in bed."

John turns away, his face a mask of misery. "I did so want to see puffins. I don't see why that's funny."

Janet's laughter stops. She looks at him for a moment, then lays a hand on his arm. "John, you are teasing me, aren't you?"

He shakes her hand away. "Of course I'm not teasing. I just wanted to see a puffin, that's all."

Janet, serious now, comes forward and puts her arms round him. "But, John, they're here."

"No, they're not. I looked."

Against his will she turns him round so that once again they are facing out to sea.

"John ..."

He waves his arm wildly, indicating the sea and the rocky pinnacle. "Not a puffin in sight."

"Not out there, John, down here."

He follows her pointing finger, brings his gaze down from the horizon to the tussocky grass almost at his feet. There, about twenty yards in front of them and stretched right out along the cliff, are puffins. Sitting, standing, poking their heads out of their burrows, puffins as far as the eye can see.

"Oh."

"I thought you were joking, John. But you were just looking too far ahead. Looking into the distance when the puffins were here all the time."

"Puffins. Oh, Janet, look at the puffins."

John's face is full of joy. Janet holds him in her arms. In the wonder of the place and the achievement, they are suddenly closer than they have been for years.

They walk along the cliff. They watch the waddling puffins. They marvel at the numbers and flight of the other seabirds. They gaze at the view. They hold hands.

"Jan, no matter what you decide …"

"What we decide …"

"We'll make it work. It can work, can't it?"

"Of course it can."

And with one final look at the puffins, they turn back downhill towards their hire car, towards the rest of their holiday and the rest of their lives, comforted by the false promise of a wonderful moment.

No-One Ever Listens

The Scilly Isles

He sat in the middle of a group of shrubs, hands clasped round his knees. He was cold. He was frightened. He was desperate.

He didn't know what was going to happen. All he knew was at least today he would not have his shins kicked, have his books thrown about, have his cap taken and thrown away, have his arms surreptitiously pinched in the dinner queue. He'd been planning this escape for days, at times he wondered if the planning was all he would do, that he would never get up the courage to do something about it but yesterday had been especially bad. Yesterday they had moved from simply pinching him to kneeing him in the groin. The pain was incredible and he could not stop the tears but that only made them laugh.

Then as he was leaving school that afternoon, he felt himself grabbed from behind, an arm went round his neck and Brian Close's hateful voice whispered in his ear.

"Enjoy tonight, cry baby. We've got a lot more

treats for you tomorrow."

Terrifying.

And then tomorrow had become today. As he got up and dressed his one thought was simply not to go to school. If he was ever to turn his plan into action it had to be now. His parents were their usual early morning snarly selves, his father left for work and his mum simply yelled goodbye to him from upstairs as he went out the door at his usual time.

He'd worked out what bus he had to catch to get to his chosen hiding place, using his father's AA road atlas to check the exact route. Before getting on the bus he'd removed his cap and blazer, crammed them into his backpack and pulled on an old jumper. He was quite proud of himself for thinking of that. Just like Sherlock Holmes or James Bond.

There wasn't as much foliage as he remembered but there was this cluster of bushes, so he had burrowed his way in there and hunkered down. Somehow, in his mind, he thought that being surrounded by a network of busy main roads would help keep him safe. A kind of traffic-filled moat around his castle.

He was tired of being picked on. He was tired of trying to explain to his parents why he was so unhappy, only to be told "Oh, do stop banging on, Sam" or "Get over it, you have to stand up for yourself".

He was tired of trying to make someone at the school take him seriously. He was tired of everything but could see no escape.

All he wanted was a little bit of peace.

"Hallo, is that Mrs Forester? ... This is Norman Mangrove. I'm the Attendance Officer at Bishop Thompson High School ... No, there's nothing wrong, well, not really. It's just that Sam didn't arrive at school this morning. Is he ill by any chance? ... Oh, I see, well, do you know where he might have gone?"

He'd sneaked into the kitchen before leaving that morning and stuffed his backpack with apples, cheese and biscuits, plus a bottle of water. He ate one of the biscuits now, peering through the foliage at the cars thundering past. The future didn't exist. All that mattered was this moment and he was safe.

"Tess, slow down, I can't understand you. You say the school called? ... Well, he probably just missed the bus ... Oh, I see, that late, no, I take your point ... Look, calm down, don't panic ... Of course he hasn't run away. Why on earth would he want to run away? ... Yes, yes, I know but all kids complain about school. It's in their genes ... Okay, look, he has his phone with him, right? ... Good, then have you tried ringing it, there's probably a perfectly sensible explanation ... No, I can't do it, they got me out of a meeting when you rang and I've got to get back there. You give him a call

and I'll ring you later to find out what he's been up to … Love you. Bye …"

His legs started to ache and he cautiously moved them to another position. He was careful not to part the protecting screen of bushes. He doubted that any of the people in the passing vehicles would notice his leg but he was taking no chances. For that reason he had not turned his phone on. He didn't want anyone trying to contact him.

"No, I'm sorry, Mrs Forester, still no sign of him … Well, if he left for school at the usual time then where else might he have gone? A friend? No, they'd be at school too, wouldn't they? A relative perhaps? … Well, if your mother lives that close then perhaps he's gone there but it rather begs the question of 'why', doesn't it?"

When he first decided to flee the persecution, he couldn't think where to go. Then he had remembered this road junction near Esher, the Scilly Isles, his dad had called it, named after some islands apparently and called that because everyone thought the collection of roundabouts was silly. There was a pub nearby and one Sunday his family with various friends had all had Sunday lunch there; someone's birthday he seemed to remember. He'd been very struck by the complexity of the roads and roundabouts and he remembered his Dad's scathing comments about what a stupid road junction it was. He reasoned that such contempt meant that it was the last place they would look for him.

"*Of course Sam's not here, Tess, he's at school … Oh, he isn't at school, I see … Well, I don't know, but he's not here … Look, calm down, Sam's a sensible boy, I'm sure there's nothing … Well, yes, of course I can see why you're worried. You poor dear. Have you spoken to Edward? … Well, that's a good idea, so have you rung Sam's mobile? … Voicemail, yes, okay … bit of a mystery but I'm sure he'll turn up … Well, I suppose you could, but … look, why not leave it to lunchtime. If he hasn't turned up by then and he's still not answering his phone, then perhaps it would be as well to call the police.*"

When he thought it was about lunchtime, he ate another biscuit and one of the apples. His mind was numb. Deep down he knew he couldn't stay where he was indefinitely but he didn't know where else to go. He simply blanked out all thoughts of the future, curled up in a tight ball in the bushes and went to sleep.

"*Emergency, which service do you require?*"

His dreams, as so often, were haunted by his failure to get anyone to listen to him.

"Don't exaggerate, Sam, you have to expect a bit of teasing when you go to school."

"We don't like sneaks in this school, Sam. You have to stand up for yourself. Give as good as you get."

"For heaven's sake, Sam, give it a rest. I'm sure it's only a bit of banter."

But it wasn't just banter. He remembered a class teacher at primary school admonishing some unruly pupils. "You may call it banter, but the person you're picking on sees it differently. It's only banter if both sides are laughing."

He can't see any reason to laugh at what has been happening to him. And the worst thing is that he is completely alone. His parents never have time to talk to him. No-one at school is interested despite their *Pupil Care policy* in big capital letters on their website. He burrows deeper into his bush and curls up even tighter. Why doesn't anyone ever listen to him? Listen to him properly.

"You've done what? Well, that's a bit over the top, isn't it, Tess. I'm sure the police have better things to do than chase after some sulky kid who's thrown a wobbly, probably because he didn't finish his homework ... Yeah, okay, okay, keep your knickers on. Let's hope they give him a good telling off when they find him ... When, I said, not if, don't be so bloody morbid. Look, got to go, see you later ... What? ... No probably not, likely to be a bit late ... Well, so what, nothing I can do is there? ... Okay, love you, bye."

When he woke he was thirsty so he drank some of the water, wishing he'd thought to bring more than one bottle. They would be starting afternoon lessons about now. He wondered if anyone had even noticed he was missing.

"*Mrs Forester? My name is Sergeant Williams. I understand your son didn't turn up for school this morning ... Yes, yes, I see. And he's what, eleven, did you say? ... Of course, now stay calm, Mrs Forester, he's probably just bunked off somewhere. We'll find him ... There's an officer on her way to you now. It would be very helpful if you have a photo of Sam that you can give her when she arrives ... No, I'm sure there's nothing like that but PC Grunning will stay with you until we find him ... Try to relax.*"

He thought he felt a few spots of rain and realised that he should have brought his anorak. Too late now. He took his cap out of his backpack and turned up his collar but luckily the rain didn't develop. He ate another biscuit and munched a bit of cheese.

"*Tess ...? It's Mum. Any news? ... Oh, I see, and she's with you now, is she? ... Well, that's something ... A photo? They're taking it seriously then. Wonder if it will be on the local news ... No, no, calm down, I'm sure he'll be back in no time ... I think that's getting a bit morbid, Tess, if you don't mind my saying so ... Okay, so do you want me to come over?*"

The feeling of security was giving way to boredom. He tried counting motorbikes that went past but he couldn't see very clearly through the bushes so he switched to lorries. That was a bit better because they were bigger but, as he admitted to himself, it was all a bit pointless.

"Mrs Forester, it's Norman Mangrove again. No news your end? ... No, I see, well we've had the police round here this afternoon. We've been asked about Sam's behaviour at school and it appears there was some kind of fracas here yesterday. Not sure what ... No, sorry, no-one's saying anything but boys will be boys ... Oh, has he? Well, it would have been helpful if he'd spoken to one of the staff here if there was a problem."

He was getting very bored. True he was safe here but he was beginning to wonder what he would do when it got dark. It must surely be the evening by now. He hadn't thought that far ahead. Could he survive out here all night or would he freeze to death? This morning he would have thought that death was preferable to facing Brian Close and his mates but now, lying in these bushes, he wasn't so sure.

"Putting his photo on the local news? Are you serious, Tess? ... Oh, I see, well, what do the police say? ... Well, they must be saying something ... Oh, well if that's what they're saying then I'd better come home ... No, I'm not grudging, I just think this is all going over the top ... Look, look, stop that, calm down, I'll come as soon as I can. It's what, four-thirty, I'll try and get away about

5.00. Okay. See you later. Love you. Bye …"

The wind was getting up and the bushes offered very little protection. He tried scraping a hole in the earth to burrow down into but only succeeded in breaking a fingernail. He ate the last biscuit.

"Bernard, it's Edward. Can we skip that meeting tonight. Tess needs me at home … No, she's not ill but Sam didn't arrive at school this morning and she's panicking, you know how they get … Gee, thanks, Bernard, that's not exactly helpful. 'Course he's not been groomed by a paedophile. Things like that don't happen to people like us … Look, I don't want to go there, okay? I'll talk to you tomorrow."

He got his blazer out of his backpack, bit crumpled but he put it on over his jumper and felt a bit warmer. He tried to think what to do next but his mind was a mess. He couldn't stay here for ever but he couldn't go back either. He was stuck. He began to cry softly.

"Hi, Tess, it's Maggie. Andrew asked me to give you a call about this weekend so we could … Tess, what is it? What's wrong? … What do you mean 'missing'? … Oh, god, Tess, you poor thing. How awful for you – what do you think's happened? … Oh, I see, well what do the police say? … And you've no idea where he's gone or why? … Look, don't worry, I'm sure he'll be okay … No, of course I don't know for certain but I'm sure … Look,

Tess, I think I'd better go. You're obviously overwrought. Let me know what happens and give me a ring if there's anything I can do."

The constant roar of the traffic was very soporific so still sobbing he curled up and went to sleep again. While he slept it began to rain in earnest.

"Okay, I'm home. This really is a nuisance. Has the little bugger turned up yet?"

When he woke again it was pitch dark. His clothes were sodden, the rain had even penetrated his blazer. He fumbled in this bag and found the last apple. That was wet too but he ate it anyway.

"To be frank, Constable, I do not like your insinuations. My son had no reason to run away. This is a happy loving home. If he does have any problems he knows he can always talk to us and we will listen to him. If anything has upset him, it's more likely to be that poncy school. I never wanted him to go there but his mother insisted."

"Actually, Edward – we both insisted. We decided. He's a high achiever, we said, we don't want him kicking around in any old school with dead-end kids."

He was shivering violently now. When he tried to move his legs he realised they had cramped. He was cold, wet and miserable. Perhaps getting beaten up by Brian Close and his friends was just something he would have to put up with. At the moment he felt he would accept anything if he could just be warm again.

"I am sorry, officer, but I cannot believe there was any problem at this school that would cause Sam to run away. We do not accept any form of bullying here and all the boys know that any member of staff is always prepared to talk through any problems they might have. I really think you need to be looking nearer home if Sam was that unhappy."

He had to move. He dragged himself out of the bush and tried to massage some warmth back into his legs. He was frightened but he had enough sense to realise that for once a retreat into sleep was not the answer. He had a vague feeling, perhaps it was something he had read somewhere, that if he slept again now he might never wake up again.

"Hallo, Sarge. I've come out into the garden where the parents can't hear me. I don't know what to say. The mother's frantic, the father's angry. They're banging on about what a happy family they are but to be honest it doesn't ring entirely true. They're all so busy blaming someone else that I think they've forgotten there's a young boy at the heart of all this … No, no, nothing like that, it's just that … oh, I don't know … there's just a sense of distance. It's almost like the kid's a concept rather than an actual child. And there's nothing we can do about that. When we find him, I'll come back to the station to

write my report and he'll just be another number, won't he ...?"

He was desperate now. He wasn't thinking straight. His dream of escape had become another prison. He had failed. Tomorrow the bullying would begin again. His parents would go on pretending to listen but in fact ignoring him. Nothing would change. But for now, he was wet, he was cold, he was hungry and he just wanted to get home.

He climbed to his feet but, even as he gathered his bits and pieces together, there was a little whisper somewhere deep down in his being. He had done this once, maybe he could do it again sometime. It would just need better planning.

BIOGRAPHY IN STEREO

The Isle of Dogs

Looking back on it now, those few months were amazing – though with hindsight I realise how lucky I was to come through unscathed.

Why did I do it? I must have been mad, but when the phone call came, I was ... how can I put it ... strapped for cash ... otherwise I might not have said 'Yes' with such enthusiasm.

On the other hand, let's be honest, when offered a job most freelance writers will say 'Yes, sure' and worry about how to deal with it later.

This call came right out of the blue, soon after six o'clock one night.

"Is that Graham Flutter?"

"Yes, in a manner of speaking."

"What d'you mean, *manner of speaking?* Are you Graham Flutter, the writer?"

"Oh, yes, most certainly."

"Good, Well, how would you like to discuss a rather lucrative writing job, Mr Flutter?"

"Who is this?"

"My name is Benjamin Sinfield and I'm looking for someone to write or, as I think you people would say, ghost, my autobiography."

"Oh, I see. Um … I'm sorry, Mr Sinfield, I don't think I know—"

"—Who I am? Don't worry. That's not a problem. The question is, do you want the job?"

Did I want the job? Any job? Is the Pope a Catholic? But it doesn't do to be too eager.

"Well, yes. Probably."

"Let's meet and discuss it."

"Certainly. When would be convenient?"

"Now."

"Now?"

"Yes, now. I'm a busy man, Mr Flutter. When I take a decision, I act on it. I'll see you here at eight. Okay?"

And so just over an hour later I was arriving at Canary Wharf station, peering at the bit of paper on which I'd hastily scribbled down his directions.

His apartment, or his pad as he called it, was stupendous. You could have fitted most of my flat into his living room and the view from the picture window looked right out over the old London Docklands. I had no idea whether the paintings on the walls and the various bowls and ornaments scattered about the room were genuine or not, but they certainly looked impressive. I sat on this amazing white leather sofa, feeling like someone in a TV advert, clutching the largest glass of single malt I had ever seen as he explained to me what he wanted.

"I'm a businessman, Mr Flutter, a successful businessman."

No surprise there. I'd worked the success bit out for myself.

"But I wasn't always successful. This," – he waved his hand around, indicating the room and everything in it – "was not always the way I lived. I was actually born here on the Isle of Dogs, in one of those awful tower blocks they put up after the war to replace homes destroyed in the Blitz."

I made the appropriate noises of appreciation.

"My dad worked in the docks for a while and my grandad was a night-watchman at Bromley-by-Bow gasworks."

Okay, I thought, *you've made your point. This is a rags to riches story. Why don't you cut to the chase.*

"But let me cut to the chase. Mine is a success story and I'd like to get it down on paper and have it published."

He paused. "I'll be honest with you, Mr Flutter, or can I call you Graham?"

I granted the favour. For a decent fee he could call me anything he liked.

"Well, then, Graham. I'm going to be 50 next year and I thought publishing the story of my life might be a nice present for the wife and kids."

I glanced round the apartment. No visible signs of any wife and kids. Benjamin saw what I was doing and smiled.

"No, they don't live here. They live in our place in the South of France."

Of course. The South of France. What was I getting myself into? And why me? I decided it was time I became positive.

"I'm sure I can do what you want, Mr Sinfield, but do you actually have a publisher lined up. In my experience that's usually the tricky part of these deals."

"Call me Benjamin," he said, "but never Ben. I don't like diminutives, okay?"

"Okay."

"Don't worry about the publisher, Graham. I do have one in mind, but I haven't told him yet."

The choice of words was not lost on me. "Well, that's great, um … Benjamin … but one other question."

"What?"

I took a deep breath, but I had to know. "Why me? I mean, there are lots of writers who …"

"You come recommended. I've seen some of

your work."

He had? Now what would that be, I wondered – my now very aptly named old TV series *Antique Detective*? My stage dramatization of *Pixie the Magic Guinea Pig* which toured in Wales, or the radio play about cross-dressing?

Whatever it was, they were all in the past. As far as writing for the media was concerned, I was yesterday's man. Then came the surprise.

"I thought your book about the *Corporate History of Throgmorton Distribution* was terrific," he went on. "I think you wrote that just after I sold the company."

"I did?"

"You did. The way you set out the company's story from its humble beginnings to a prominent place on the Stock Exchange was a master of spin. I particularly liked the way you put a neat gloss on where the original capital had come from."

I hadn't known I'd put a neat gloss on where the original capital had come from. I'd simply worked from the briefing notes the HR director had sent me. By that stage I was snatching any writing job which floated into view.

Benjamin smiled, or at least the line of his lips extended a little to each side. "Now let me just check a couple of things, Graham. You're not married right?"

"Right."

"Not now, at least."

"Pardon?"

"My information is that your wife ran off with a television repair man but not before she had cleaned out your joint savings account."

"How the hell do you know that?"

The lips twitched again. "I always do my research before offering anyone a job."

"So all that guff about liking my work …"

"Is absolutely true. I did like that book, and I am certain you're the writer I want. And I daresay you'd welcome the chance of earning some decent money, wouldn't you?"

"Of course, but …"

"So let's continue. You currently live alone, yes?"

"Yes, but …"

"And no close ties at present?"

"No, but …"

"So no problem about devoting all your time to this project?"

I gave in. "None at all."

"Good. I want it completed as quickly as possible. Now then. The question of your fee."

I perked up. Intrusive sod he might be, but in my current financial state this was the bit I had really come to hear.

"How much do you charge?"

I thought furiously. It was the old dilemma, you don't want to pitch it too low and undersell yourself. On the other hand you don't want to be too greedy and lose the work.

"Well ..." I said cautiously, "it rather depends on the client."

Benjamin nodded. "I thought it might. How about five thousand pounds down, another ten when you deliver the first draft, with a final bonus of five K when we publish it?

For a moment it seemed as though the magical view of Docklands had gone into soft focus. The single malt took on an extra flavour as I grappled with what I had just heard. I couldn't take it in. Two hours ago I was worrying about how to pay the gas bill and suddenly I was being offered twenty thousand pounds.

I glanced over my shoulder in case Father Christmas had arrived unobserved but no, silly of me, these apartments didn't have any chimneys. I turned back to see Benjamin regarding me with amusement.

"I'll take that as a 'yes' then," he said. "Okay, let's get down to business."

I gathered my bemused thoughts together. "Yes. Business. Now how do you want to work? You'll obviously have to give me all the background but that doesn't have to be chronological. We'll need to organise some sessions together – I'll bring a recording machine and then you can …"

"No recording machine." The interruption was clipped and unequivocal.

"Pardon?"

"I said no recording machine. I do not want my voice recorded. We will organise a series of meetings. I will talk, you will take notes."

"I don't do shorthand."

"Then write quickly, but no recording. Right?"

"Right." It would be tedious but for twenty grand I could put up with a bit of tedium. "When do you want to start?"

"Tomorrow evening. I suggest we meet twice a week."

"I'm free during the day."

"I'm not. All our meetings will be in the evening and you will not tell anyone about them. Is that clear? If I find you've spoken to anyone about this, the deal's off."

"Yes, but what about my agent? I'll have to tell him. He'll want to see the contract."

"There will be no contract. I will give you the first five thousand now and the rest as we agreed. Your agent hasn't been doing much for you recently so I suggest you forget all about him."

"No contract, but you'll give me five thousand pounds now?"

"Yes."

"That's very trusting of you."

He gave me the pseudo smile again. "Trust doesn't come into it, Graham. People never let me down, if you see what I mean."

I remembered what he'd said about growing up in another part of the Isle Of Dogs and I saw what he meant. There was clearly much more to this job than just a vanity biography but in my current situation and for that kind of fee I was prepared to write what I was told and leave it at that. However, like many freelance writers, I tend to see real life in terms of plot structure, and I have a strong sense of self preservation.

"Okay, no formal contract. No agent. But I do want a written agreement."

"You want what?"

"Just a simple bit of paper, signed by both of us, saying that you've commissioned me to write the story of your life for this fee. That's all."

"Why the hell do you want that?"

"For my own protection. What if you got run over or something and I have to explain to your wife or your solicitor how it is I'm sitting on a large wad of your money?"

"You're a cheerful sod, aren't you? Nothing's going to happen to me."

"I hope not, but I have to cover my back."

There was a brief pause and then Benjamin gave me the thin smile again. "You've got a lot of cheek, but I like you. All right, you can have your letter, but you write it. Keep it short. If I'm happy with it, I'll sign it. And then I'll keep it."

"You'll keep it?"

"Yes, I'll send it to my solicitor so if I hypothetically get run over then when they sort out my estate you'll be in the clear."

For a moment we looked at each other then I nodded.

"Okay." I paused for a moment then decided to go for broke. "And I want expenses."

He shook his head in disbelief. "What expenses?"

"Paper, printer cartridges, oh, yes, and if I'm coming here twice a week you can top up my Oyster card too."

For a moment I wondered if I'd gone too far but then he laughed. "You cheeky sod. All right, you've got it. I like a man with spirit. Anything else while we're about it?"

"Yes, what's the name of this malt? It's a stunner."

"It's Talisker from the Isle of Skye – long way from the Isle of Dogs, yeah?"

"You bet."

"Okay, Graham, let's shake. You've got a deal, printer cartridges and all."

We shook hands and I made my way back to my flat in West Hampstead clutching a cheque for five thousand pounds, feeling slightly shell-shocked. Ironically the thing that worried me most was the timing. A too-good-to-be-true deal popping up just when I was getting seriously desperate smacked of a bad TV script, but the five thousand pounds was real enough so I decided to go with the flow. I'd turn his fantasies into printed reality but keep my eyes open. The following morning I paid the cheque into my bank account and bought a bottle of Talisker.

It was on my fifth visit to see Benjamin that things started to get complicated. It was just after half past six and I'd set out on the short walk from Canary Wharf station when I was suddenly aware of someone coming up behind me. I began to turn but as I did so someone caught my arm and then someone else grabbed the other arm and a quiet voice muttered in my ear. "Don't say anything, Mr Flutter. Just keep walking, nice and quiet, round this next corner."

The tightness of the grip on my arm and the soft silkiness of the voice made me think that the best thing I could do was not to say anything and just keep walking, nice and quiet, round the next corner. My mind, however, was racing. I was clearly about to get mugged but they hadn't chosen well. I had fifteen pounds and a few pence on me and my watch was a ten quid job from the local discount store.

But they weren't interested in my watch. It was me, they wanted. Round the corner was a black car with tinted windows. It was so like a piss-take of a Hollywood movie that if it hadn't been me being hustled quietly and efficiently into the back seat, I would have laughed out loud.

One man got in beside me, the other got into the front and as the car pulled away from the kerb, I finally found my voice.

"What the hell's going on?"

Okay, I know it's not a terribly original line and I know that, as writer, I should have been able to come up with something better, but at the time that simple question summed up everything I wanted to know.

"Don't worry, Mr Flutter," said the man beside me. "No-one's going to hurt you – at least I don't think they are. We're just taking you to see Jeremy. He wants to have a little chat."

"I don't know anyone called Jeremy."

"It doesn't matter. He knows you."

Fortunately it was a short journey, not enough time to get really frightened. We pulled up outside one of those old pubs that feature in films from the 1930s. The view from outside told you that inside there would be a lot of wood and brass rails.

I was helped, reasonably gently, out of the car and came up with yet another immortal line.

"Where are we?"

My companions seemed surprised by the question. "We're at Mudchute," said one of them, "down the bottom of the Isle of Dogs. Thought you was a Londoner?"

"I am, but there's a lot of London and I don't know this bit."

"Oh, right. Well, this is The Raven, one of Jeremy's pubs. We'll go in round the back. He's looking forward to meeting you."

The upstairs room I was ushered into was large with high windows and continued the 1930s film theme. There was a bar in one corner and a pool table up one end. One of the men playing pool, stopped as we entered. He came across and thrust out his hand.

"Hi, I'm Jeremy. You must be Graham."

"Well, yes, but …"

"Have a seat, Graham. Drink?" He snapped his fingers. "Get Graham a scotch. Talisker single malt. That's what he likes."

I sat down rather shakily. This was rapidly becoming unreal. Jeremy sat down opposite me. His sleeves were rolled up and I was fascinated by his forearms. I had never seen so much hair. I wondered if he had to comb them. Then I saw something else. Nestling into the hair on his right arm, like a cat in a warm basket, was a very curious tattoo. It looked like a water buffalo and a small deer having energetic sex.

I lifted my eyes and looked at the face of the man opposite me. A hard face, plenty of lines and they didn't look like laughter lines. The eyes were a cold blue. A large glass was put in front of me. Jeremy's glass held a white liquid that looked a bit like milk. He saw me looking at it and smiled.

"I used to like the hard stuff too but then I got this ulcer and, well, you know how it is … now all I drink is milk."

I took a deep breath.

"Who are you and what am I doing here?"

Jeremy nodded slowly. "So I was right. The bastard hasn't mentioned me, has he?"

"Which bastard did you have in mind?" I asked though an awful suspicion was beginning to dawn.

"My brother, Benjamin. That bastard. You didn't even know he had a brother, did you?"

I shook my head.

"Well, he does. Me. I'm the oldest. Ben's two years younger."

"He prefers to be called Benjamin. He doesn't like

diminutives."

"I don't give a sod what he likes. He's trying to give me the run around again, isn't he?"

"I don't quite know…"

"Look, let's cut to the chase …"

Well, at least the brothers had that much in common.

"Ben's hired you to write his autobiography, right?"

"Well, I don't know if I should discuss …"

"Right?"

"Yes, right."

"And has he mentioned me? How I gave him his start? How two brothers from a difficult background both made good in their own ways?"

"Well …"

"'Course he hasn't. You didn't even know I existed, did you?"

"Well … No …"

"Exactly. I bet you've been given the 'local boy makes good' stuff. How he pulled himself up by his own bootstraps. How he made a few deals, maybe some of them a little shady, but then he started to make money and now all the deals are legit. That's about the size of it, isn't it?"

I shrugged. There didn't seem much point in dissembling any further. Jeremy clearly knew all about it.

"Benjamin made no secret of some of those early deals. In fact I think he's quite proud of them. He wants me to express them in such a way that doesn't actually say they were slightly dodgy but just let the implication hang in the air, so to speak."

"Hang in the air, my arse. There were no slightly dodgy deals."

"Oh. Are you saying he's inventing a purple past to add some frisson to the book?"

"I don't know about frisson. I do know it's a load of bollocks." He leaned forward. "What I'm about to tell you, Graham, is confidential. I strongly recommend that you never repeat it outside these four walls. All right?"

I nodded.

"Let me hear you say it."

"All right. Whatever you tell me will not be repeated outside these four walls."

"You swear that on your mother's grave?"

"My mother's not dead."

"Oh, for Christ's sake, don't get bogged down in detail. Your Dad's grave, your Granny's grave, anyone's bloody grave. Do you swear it?"

I took a deep breath. "I do. I swear it on the grave of my great-great grandfather who was killed in the Boer War and is buried at Braamfontein Cemetery in

South Africa."

Jeremy gave me a long look but let it pass. "Okay, then. Now listen, there were no dodgy deals. Anyway dodgy deals are quite respectable today. Banks and politicians do them all the time."

"Sure. So what?"

"Just this. Brother Ben's little empire was built on the proceeds of a number of … what shall we say … decidedly antisocial activities. The kind that if you were caught, would make you a guest of Her Majesty for a few years."

I looked at him. "How antisocial?"

"Well, you know how it is. A little robbery here, a bit of protection there, all edged round with a bit of creative accounting."

"Crime you mean. You're saying he's a criminal? A robber? A burglar? A gangster? Whatever the term is."

Jeremy looked rather pained. "Not a burglar, Graham. That's not very polite. We never nipped down to Sunningdale to break into an old lady's house to nick her wedding ring. That wouldn't be very nice, now would it?"

"And the odd robbery and a bit of protection's nice, is it?"

Jeremy leaned across the table. "You have to remember, Graham, that this is all in the past. We haven't done a job for years. Personally, I don't need to. I've got a nice little business empire going and it does me fine."

"What sort of empire?"

"Pubs. Betting shops. Cafés. Couple of drinks companies. All perfectly legit and above board."

"And what about below board?"

Jeremy shook his head. "Not any more, Graham, simply isn't worth it. There's so many fiddles on the right side of the law. Why take the risk?"

I thought for a minute. "How does all this link in with your brother?"

"It links in with my brother, Graham, because Ben is a lying sod. He didn't get his start-up capital from dodgy deals. He got it from robbery and ... well ... the other bits and pieces. Just like me. Well, with me actually. We still worked together in those days. These days ... well ... these days we don't really talk."

"So he's been lying to me."

"I don't know if he's been lying or not. I do know he's been pretty selective with the truth."

"There's good precedent for that these days."

"Sure, but now things have changed."

"How?"

"He's about to let the family down and we can't be having that."

"Let the family down? How do you mean, let down?"

"My family have lived in this part of London for generations. We're known round here. The bloody Germans tried to bomb us out – we didn't go. When I was a young man the police tried to fit us up – it didn't work. We're still here. And now Benjamin is planning to sell out."

"You mean he's going to grass you up and destroy your manor?"

Jeremy took a hefty swig of milk and sighed deeply. "You've been watching too much telly, Graham. No-one talks like that in real life."

"What's he about to do that's so bad then?"

"He's planning to go into politics. No-one in the family has ever sunk as low as that before."

"He's never mentioned politics to me."

"You see, I told you. Selective. Ben fancies being a public figure. That's what this autobiography is all about. He needs his image tidying up a bit. He needs … oh, what's the word?"

"A profile?"

"That's it. He needs a profile."

"But he told me he wants the story of his life written down as a 50th birthday present for his wife and kids."

Jeremy gave a snort of derision. 'Snort of derision'

was a phrase I had written several times but I had never known how it really sounded before.

"Kids? Ben? You've got to be joking. Ben hasn't got any kids. He can't stand them."

"Oh, I see. But he has got a wife, I presume?"

"Oh, yes," said Jeremy slowly, "he has certainly got a wife."

At the time I did not fully appreciate his emphasis on the indefinite article.

"Okay, wife but no kids, so maybe you're right. Maybe he is just trying to clean up his image, but Ben … um … Benjamin? Politics? What party is he standing for."

"I don't give a sod what party. They're all as dirty as each other. I just don't want him besmirching the family name. That's all."

"But how can you stop him?"

"Well, I can start by making sure his manicured past is put into context and that's where you come in."

"Me?"

"You."

"But what can I do? I can't change the facts."

Jeremy sighed. "Don't be naïve, Graham. You're not dealing in facts. You're helping Ben massage his image."

"Well, yes, okay, but it's his image. He's paying

me, he's going to read what I write. I can't do anything about that."

"Maybe not. But there's another point of view and you can do something about that."

"I can?"

"You can. So let's talk about our deal."

"What deal?"

He sighed again. "Why d'you take on this job, Graham?"

"Well, I'm a freelance writer. That's what I do and it sounded interesting."

"So it was nothing to do with the fact that you're broke, you owe money all over the place and if you don't pay all your back rent by the end of the month you'll be kicked out of your flat and be on the street."

I was silent. It was seriously scary what these people knew about me.

Jeremy saw my look and went straight on. "So Ben's offer was good timing from your point of view. But that wasn't chance. You were desperate for money, he has the money so that means he's in control. He likes being in control."

I swallowed. "And now I suppose I've blown it?"

Jeremy suddenly became very friendly. "Blown it, Graham? Not at all. In fact it's just improved."

"What has?"

"Your financial situation."

"It has?" I was beginning to lose track of the plot.

"Sure it has. You've already got Ben's deal, now you're going to have mine too."

"Your what?"

"My story. The book you're going to write for me."

"I am?"

"You are."

"I'm not sure that's ethical."

"This is London. Ethics is the next county along." He paused. "That's a joke by the way."

"Oh. Yes. Fine." But I didn't feel like laughing. I wasn't sure I liked the way this conversation was going. On the other hand, I didn't seem to have much say over its direction.

Jeremy went on. "You see, Graham, I've decided that I'd also like to have my life story published. Give me the chance to put a few things straight, and my take on the life of the Sinfield brothers should neatly scupper Ben's political ambitions."

"I don't know what Benjamin's going to say."

"Ben's not going to know. Unless you tell him and I don't think you'd be that stupid, would you?"

Things were rapidly moving from the surreal to the frankly impossible and I was struggling to keep some sort of grasp on reality.

"Well, when would you want to do this? I'm

already meeting Benjamin two evenings a week."

"We can meet here during the day. Then you can go on to Ben in the evening. That way you won't need to sting me for a new Oyster card as well."

I retreated onto safer ground. "Do you have a publisher lined up?"

"Not yet. But we'll find one when we need one."

I swallowed and for a moment toyed with the fantasy of the chairman of one of the Big Four publishers being invited to have a ride in the black car with tinted windows and being given a dry sherry, or whatever he or she drank, in the room above The Raven. Then reality kicked back in. I had a job to do. Well, two jobs actually. I just hoped I could keep them from colliding.

"Okay then, let's sort out the details. How do you want to work? You'll obviously have to give me all the background but …"

"No recording machines. You'll have to …"

I sighed. "Yes I know. You don't want your voice recorded. You will talk, I will take notes, writing as quickly as I can."

"That's about it."

"And you don't want me to tell anyone about all this until we are ready to publish."

"You've got it, Graham. And whatever Ben is paying you, I will match it. Just one thing."

"What?"

"Don't try and take me for a ride. Don't give Ben any information about me, don't exaggerate what he's paying you or anything like that. I'm sure you'd find it hard to use a keyboard if all your fingers was broken."

I shivered. "I wouldn't dream of it."

"Good."

"But I do want a written agreement."

"You want what?"

"That's what your brother said but we sorted it. All I need is a simple bit of paper, signed by both of us, saying that you've commissioned me to write the story of your life for this fee. That's all."

"And why would you want that?"

"As I told your brother, for my own protection. If something happens to you I don't want to have to explain to your wife or …"

"What about my wife?" Suddenly he was leaning across the table, his face thrust close to mine.

"Nothing. I just meant …"

"You leave my wife out of this, okay?"

"Sure. Sure."

"So what's all this agreement stuff?"

"Just a simple statement of what you're paying me and for what. Then if there's ever a problem with … with your … er … friends then I can show why I've got all this money from you."

There was a brief pause and then Jeremy sat back and grinned. "You're a cheeky bugger, but I like you. Okay, you can have your letter but I'll keep it. And …"

I sighed. "I know, you'll pass it on to your solicitor for safe keeping."

Jeremy nodded. "Right. But you're not getting any expenses. Ben can cover those. Okay?"

"Okay."

And so began a very strange time. Twice a week I'd leave home after lunch and take the Jubilee Line from West Hampstead to Canary Wharf. There the black car would be waiting to whisk me down to Mudchute where I'd spend around three hours with Jeremy making notes as fast as I could as he unravelled the story of his life.

Then I'd have a quick snack in the bar of The Raven and the black car would take me back to Canary Wharf where I would walk round the corner and spend another three hours listening to Benjamin and writing furiously again. Then I'd catch a late train back to West Hampstead.

The following day I'd do a series of exercises for my aching wrist and then spend the time before the next set of meetings typing up my notes on the lives of the two brothers.

As any writer knows, memory is a totally unreliable source and the brothers were no exception. The emerging tales of their two lives bore little relationship to each other but even allowing for the natural faults of memory it was obvious that there was a lot of massaging of the truth going on. Interestingly, but perhaps not surprisingly, most of the massaging came from Benjamin. Jeremy was far more honest, though more than a little vague about the details of the various events (he called them operations) that he and Benjamin had indulged in to build their initial capital base.

It soon became clear that there was a permanent rift between the brothers. Benjamin never mentioned Jeremy's existence to me and my attempts to probe the reason for this estrangement with Jeremy were ignored. Once I tried to pump the driver of the black car who, I had learned, answered to the name of Mudguards, but got nowhere. All he would say was:

"Word to the wise, Graham. Never talk to the boss about his brother or his missus. Not if you prefer having two working legs, that is."

As the weeks passed, I became more and more wary about both brothers. Sitting with them, listening to them talk, it became apparent that there was a lot of subtext underneath the stories they were giving me. Benjamin never referred directly to anything dishonest, other than an occasional reference to some tax dodge or other, but when I came to piece it all together, quite a lot of it didn't add up. I remembered Jeremy's comments about the origins of their start-up capital and came to the conclusion that my job was to make it add up, to present a squeaky clean image of Benjamin to the world while hinting gently at a colourful past. I was always very polite with Benjamin. There was something cold about him that made me feel that you wouldn't want him on the opposite team.

Jeremy sparked the same sort of feeling but it was more upfront. I had no doubt that to get on the wrong side of Jeremy would mean a car ride with Mudguards and 'the boys' that they would enjoy more than I would. There was a simmering level of violence in Jeremy that scared the hell out of me though it must be said he was never anything but polite and after that first brief reference to the possible state of my fingers, no threats were ever made. Mind you, I was pretty careful not to give any cause for them to be made.

After several weeks I felt I had enough material to begin the first drafts so our regular meetings tailed off and I began writing in earnest. I discovered the best way of working was to spend the morning on

Benjamin's book and the afternoon on Jeremy's. That way I could develop the stories in parallel because, even though they were different, they followed the same timescale and it was interesting having two takes.

I work fast so it wasn't long before I had a rough draft for each book but then things started to go a little odd – that is, even odder than they were already. I was about to begin the first revision when I had a message from Jeremy to say he wanted to read what I'd done so far to "see how it's shaping up".

I don't normally like people seeing what I'm writing until I have a draft I'm happy with, but the brothers were not normal clients, and Jeremy hadn't had the advantage of reading my *Corporate History of Throgmorton Distribution,* so I printed out his version and took it along to The Raven.

When I arrived, I was taken into a back room of the pub where I had not been before. Jeremy was sitting behind a desk, a rather incongruous sight, and he waved me to the chair in front of it. Then the first odd thing happened. As I went to sit down I noticed something on the seat, and to my surprise I saw it was a shotgun.

Jeremy saw me hesitate and peered over the desk. "Oh, sorry, I forgot that was there. We had a business meeting in here earlier."

I tried not to let my mind dwell on the concept of a business meeting facilitated with a shotgun.

"Just move it," said Jeremy. "Stick it over there."

I hesitated and Jeremy made an impatient gesture so I gingerly picked up the gun. It was heavier than I expected and the stock was a beautiful polished wood, warm to the touch.

"I thought shotguns always had their barrels side by side."

Jeremy laughed. "You watch too many movies, I told you. No, some guns do, this one doesn't. It's a Beretta – an under and over gun. Just pop it on the shelf over there. I'll lock it up later."

I moved over to the shelves while Jeremy watched me with amusement.

"Don't worry, Graham, it's not loaded. It won't bite."

"I've never held a shotgun before."

"Really? I grew up with them myself."

I laid the gun down and came back to the desk. Jeremy took the manuscript I handed him and settled down to read. However, he only read two or three chapters and then stopped.

"That'll do for the moment," he said, "looks like it's shaping up fine."

I was a bit surprised but my commercial instincts were still functioning. "Well, if you're happy then could I have the second stage of the fee, please?"

"What? Oh, yes, of course." He scribbled a cheque and pushed it across the desk.

Five minutes later I was on my way back to the station wondering what that meeting had really been about. As a writer I can spot an unnecessary scene at a hundred paces and that episode in Jeremy's office left me feeling uneasy.

Although, to the best of my knowledge, Benjamin still knew nothing about Jeremy's book, I decided that as one brother had seen an early draft then the other brother should also see his, so I phoned Benjamin and suggested it.

When I arrived at his apartment Benjamin poured me a large Talisker – I was getting quite a taste for it by this time – and settled me down in the white leather sofa while he read the manuscript. He read a lot faster than Jeremy and I could tell from the occasional grunt that he was not displeased with what he was reading.

Naturally Jeremy was not mentioned in Benjamin's book. I'd made a passing reference to other members of the extended family but having put my famous gloss on the origins of his start-up capital, the story moved rapidly on from his early life.

When he had finished reading he handed the manuscript back to me and nodded his approval.

"Very nice," he said, "reads well, doesn't it?"

"Local boy makes good," I said.

"Local boy makes very good," said Benjamin and laughed. "And local boy is about to make even better."

Benjamin had never mentioned his political ambitions to me so I didn't comment. I had to struggle a bit sometimes to remember what I'd heard from Jeremy that Benjamin should not know that I knew. I didn't want trouble. I just wanted to finish the job, collect my fee and forget all about the Isle of Dogs.

"Right then," said Benjamin, "I guess you'd like the second part of your fee."

"Well ..." I said.

"I've got it right here," and he took a cheque out of his pocket. I put my hand out to take it but then he hesitated.

"Graham," he said, "I would like you to do me a little favour."

I was instantly alert. I was not easy about the kind of favours either of the brothers might ask me. On the other hand neither of them were the kind of men who would take 'no' for an answer.

"What kind of favour?" I asked cautiously.

"I'd like you to look after something for me, just for a few weeks."

"What sort of something?"

"Oh, just a little bit of cash. I've got it here at the moment but I might be having some visitors shortly and I'd like it somewhere else for a while."

This sounded very dodgy to me but I couldn't see any way to refuse.

"How much cash and what do you want me to do with it?"

"Oh, it's only around two hundred grand or so …"

I gulped.

"… and I think the best thing would be for you to open a number of savings accounts, post office, building societies and so on. Pop a bit in each, not the same amount each time, don't make it too obvious. That'll keep it safe until I need it back. Here, I've put together a list of places for you to use, save you the trouble of doing the research."

And this keeps your name away from it, I thought, *but makes sure you know where it's all gone.* Aloud I said, "You'd trust me with that much cash?"

"Of course," said Benjamin, "you wouldn't let me down, Graham, would you?" And again I got that thin smile.

Not for the first time I wondered which of the brothers was the more dangerous, Jeremy with his shotgun or Benjamin with his smile.

"But won't it look a bit dodgy? Me suddenly having all this money?"

"No problem," said Benjamin, "I've prepared a number of betting slips for you showing you've been lucky on the horses lately."

I swallowed. Two hundred thousand pounds sounded like a lot of horses to me but there was clearly no way out of this.

"Well … all right … I suppose … When d'you want to do this?"

"Oh, now," said Benjamin, "I'll go and get the cash. Won't be a moment."

He went out of the room and left to myself I got up and wandered around. I'd seen from my first visit that some of the pictures on the walls were serious art and now I went and looked at them more closely. Below the pictures were some photographs on a shelf, one of Benjamin in a business suit in what looked like a board room, another of him with a group of other men and another where he was obviously making a speech. Then I noticed a corner of a picture frame poking out from behind one of the others. Just by way of idle curiosity I eased it out and looked at it.

It was a photo of a woman in a bikini lying on a lounger beside a swimming pool. From the intensity of the light I knew it wasn't in England. I peered closer and then suddenly I couldn't believe my eyes.

I heard the sound of Benjamin returning and hastily put the picture back in its hiding place. When he came back into the room I was staring out at the old docks through that huge picture window.

"Here we are," he said. "Money, betting slips and the list of the best places to open the accounts. I've put them in this little attaché case to make them easier to carry. Now then, I think it would be a good idea to organise a car home for you, yes? Don't want that much cash kicking around on the Jubilee Line, do we?"

When I got home that night I poured myself a large Talisker and thought very hard. Occasionally I checked through some of the notes I'd made of the first conversations with the brothers but mostly I just sat and thought. I had no doubt that I would need to move very carefully from now on.

By the time I went to bed I still wasn't sure what my next move should be but the following morning my phone rang and it was Mudguards with a message from Jeremy. I listened carefully and then knew exactly what I had to do.

Ten days later I got out of a taxi in West End Lane but as I walked up the steps towards my flat two rather large men appeared each side of me. For a moment it seemed like a replay of the evening when

Jeremy's boys had first taken me to The Raven, but these two particular boys played on a different team.

"Excuse me, sir. Are you Mr Graham Flutter?"

"Yes, you could say that."

"I'm Detective Sergeant Wilkins of the Metropolitan Police, this is Detective Constable Arbuthnot."

A couple of ID cards were flashed in front of my nose.

"How can I help you, gentlemen?"

"Graham Flutter, I'm arresting you for the murder of Benjamin Sinfield. You do not have to say anything, but it may harm your defence if you do not mention when questioned something which you later rely on in court. Anything you do say may be given in evidence. Do you understand?"

"Yes, but I haven't killed anybody."

"Just come with us, sir."

"Hang on a minute. Let me see your warrant cards again."

They both sighed but produced their cards and this time I had a really good look.

"Happy now, sir?"

"Quite happy, thank you." Both cards looked genuine but the mere fact that they'd shown them to me again without just grabbing me a hustling me away convinced me that they were genuine policemen and not some friends of Jeremy's.

At the police station I was asked if I wanted a solicitor, but I said that for the time being I didn't think it was necessary. This surprised DS Wilkins but clearly caused him less trouble so the recorder was switched on and the interview began.

"Mr Flutter, can you tell us where you were on the evening of Friday 7th July?"

"Certainly. I was in The Russian Tea Room."

"The what?"

"The Russian Tea Room. It's a restaurant in New York."

"You were in New York?"

"Yes, I flew over on Wednesday 5th. I've been working on a book, well a couple of books actually, and I thought a few days away would give me some space to polish the text."

"Did you tell anyone where you were going?"

"No one to tell, Sergeant. I live alone. I have no one, so I'm a free agent."

"Did you meet anyone while you were in New York?"

"Lots of people but specifically at the Russian Tea Room I was having dinner with Macdonald Wishart, who I hope will represent me in the States."

"Is he a lawyer?"

"No, a literary agent. I was not aware I might

need a lawyer."

"So you weren't in London on Friday 7th?"

"Well, now, Sergeant, a writer can be anywhere he wants in his head but he, like the rest of humanity, is limited to one physical place at a time."

"There's something very odd going on here."

"There certainly is. Don't you think you should tell me what's happened and why you think I may have killed Benjamin Sinfield, who, incidentally, is the subject of one the books I'm writing."

The sergeant eyed me thoughtfully for a moment. "Sometime during the evening of Friday 7th July, Benjamin Sinfield was killed by two blasts from a shotgun in his apartment at Canary Wharf. We'd like to compare your fingerprints with those on the stock and the barrel of the gun."

"Oh, I see. Well, then please go ahead. I suspect you'll find they are my prints, but I'm equally sure you've checked and found the gun is not registered in my name – if indeed it is registered at all."

"Oh, it's registered all right. To Johnny Kendrick, who goes by the street name of Mudguards, from the Raven pub, Mudshute on the Isle of Dogs."

"There you are then …"

"And who also says it was stolen from there shortly after your visit to that pub a week or so earlier. Are you telling me you've never seen this gun?"

"Not at all. I have seen it and I've handled it ..."

"Aha ..."

"But not on Friday 7th July because ..."

"... because you were in New York."

"Precisely."

"We will check this, Mr Flutter."

"I'm sure you will."

"I'm particularly interested in how you were in New York when there is no trace of your having left the country."

"I presume you were looking for Graham Flutter."

"Of course."

"Then that explains it. My passport is in the name of Giles Franklin, my real name."

"Your real name?"

"Yes. Graham Flutter is my pen name. A lot of writers do that. It saves unwelcome publicity. It's all legal."

A hint of a smile almost touched Sergeant Wilkins' face. "Would I be right in supposing that the decision to go to New York at this time was not a casual one?"

"You would be right."

"Did you know what was going to happen?"

"No. Not specifically, but I was pretty sure something was being planned and I thought it would be a sensible precaution to have a cast iron alibi just in case. These days the immigration requirements of the States are so severe that it will be easy to check I was there and only left there last night."

"I am sure it will, Mr Flutter. But what made you think something might happen?"

Secure in the knowledge that I'd been safely the other side of passport control when Benjamin was killed, and secure in the knowledge that Benjamin's little attaché case was at the bottom of the Hudson River, I had no hesitation in telling the Sergeant the whole story, well most of it anyway. How the unnecessary meeting at the Raven with Jeremy had bothered me. How I'd examined the sequence of events from the point of view of a writer plotting a script and realised the only possible purpose of that scene was to make sure my prints were on the gun. The message from Jeremy, which told me to meet him on Maritime Quay near the Masthouse Terrace Pier at the southern end of the Isle of Dogs at 11.00 pm on that Friday night, had confirmed my suspicions so I decided to be safely out of the way during the time in question.

"You seem quite relaxed about all this, Mr Flutter."

"Believe me, Sergeant, I'd be considerably less relaxed if Jeremy were asking me these questions, rather than you – I'm rather fond of my fingers."

"Well he can't. He's dead too."

"*Is he?*"

"But we're not looking at you for that one, Mr Flutter. He was stabbed by Benjamin's wife later that same night."

"And is she in custody too?"

"She certainly is and has admitted killing him but says it was self-defence."

"I see."

"She also says she received an anonymous phone call warning her that Jeremy was threatening her husband so she went to confront him."

"The husband?"

"No, Jeremy. Things got heated and she stabbed him."

I nodded wisely. "Interesting story. Seems to have a few gaps in it though."

"Yes, it does." Sergeant Wilkins looked me straight in the eye. "We're not even sure Rosamund Sinfield is Benjamin Sinfield's wife, though that's what she claims."

"I don't understand."

"I suspect you do, Mr Flutter. Two brothers, same surname. Wife, same surname."

"Oh, I see, you think this Rosamund might really be Jeremy's wife."

"She might. In fact she is, we've checked. So the question is – what's going on?"

I leaned back in my chair. "I wouldn't know, but if I were writing this for television then I might have made Rosamund the actual wife of Jeremy but then develop the plot in such a way that she came to prefer Benjamin. Probably attracted by his more affluent lifestyle, or something like that. Then you've also got a motive for the bad feeling between the brothers."

"Bit of a cliché, don't you think?"

"I certainly do. Doubt you'd get it through an astute script editor, unless you had a long track record and could put a bit of spin on it."

"But you think this is what happened, do you?"

"I've no idea, sergeant. But again, if I were writing this, I would need something to make a connection, to make it clear to the audience whose wife she really was."

Sergeant Wilkins nodded thoughtfully. "Something like a very unusual tattoo on his arm and on her thigh, you mean? Something like that?"

I thought back to the photo I'd found in Benjamin's flat. It certainly had been an unusual tattoo. "That might work," I said, "and then of course you'd need a fall guy, someone that Jeremy could set up to take the blame for his brother's murder."

"Why would Jeremy want to murder his brother?"

"Okay, so, let's think the plot line through properly. You have to do that these days you know, script editors aren't a pushover."

"I'm sure they're not. So, getting back to this plot."

"This fictional plot. Well, the wife's infidelity might not be motive enough on its own so maybe you need to chuck in something else. Perhaps Benjamin stole something from Jeremy and that proved the last straw."

Sergeant Wilkins was watching me closely. "Something like two hundred thousand pounds perhaps?"

I thought for a moment. "Yes, that might do it. You could work it so that Benjamin knew where Jeremy had stashed his little nest egg and just helped himself to it."

"Very interesting. Well, since you mention it, we found a letter in Benjamin's apartment apparently written by you and demanding two hundred thousand pounds as a price of your silence about the source of all his wealth. Any truth in that?"

"None whatsoever. But it's starting to look like quite a nice little script, isn't it, Sergeant. Baddies fighting amongst themselves, getting their comeuppance. Script editors like that sort of plot."

"But this is real life, Mr Flutter."

"Ah, well, I don't know much about that, Sergeant?" I thought for a moment. "This blackmail letter I'm meant to have written …"

"It was quite clear. It even had a list of accounts where you had, allegedly, instructed Benjamin to pay the money into."

"Have you found any such accounts?"

"No, we haven't. Just your two bank accounts, your current account and a savings account with just under thirty thousand in it."

"Ah, but I can explain that."

"You don't have to. We've also seen your letters of agreement with the brothers to ghost-write their respective life stories."

"Have you indeed? Then you must have been in my flat."

"Yes, we have. With a proper search warrant, I might add." He paused and I could have sworn I saw the hint of a smile touch his mouth. Not a Benjamin type thin smile, more the struggle of a man trying to stop himself laughing.

"Just one thing, Mr Flutter. When we entered your flat we found the two agreements on your desk, very handy for anyone to see. It was almost as though you were expecting visitors."

"Must have forgotten to put them away before I went abroad."

"You must indeed. And they appeared to be prints of photos."

"That's right. Taken on my phone. The brothers each wanted to keep them but I thought I ought to have a copy myself so in a quiet moment I just took a picture."

"I see."

"This blackmail letter, Sergeant, was it printed or handwritten?"

"Printed but signed, apparently by you."

"Ah. Well then, I suppose in a script the next thing to do would be to get a handwriting expert to have a look at that signature."

"Yes, it probably would, but I've a feeling that might be a waste of time.

"Really?"

"Yes. We did check the printer type – laser, inkjet and so on – and the letter didn't come from the machine in your flat."

"Rather looks like someone was trying to frame me, then."

"It does rather." There was a brief pause and then the Sergeant stood up. "This interview terminated at fourteen twenty-three. You're free to go, Mr Flutter. We will, as I said, be checking that you really did go to New York …"

"Oh, I did."

"And now I know about your passport I am sure that will be confirmed which is why I'm letting you go. The only thing is – I can't decide if you are very lucky or very clever."

"Neither really, Sergeant. But I am a good writer, especially on plots."

We walked together to the door of the police station and as I turned to go down the steps he called after me.

"Any ideas what you'll spend the two hundred grand on, Mr Flutter?"

I turned and smiled at him. "I've never thought about it, sergeant. I'm never likely to have that kind of money, am I?" And I went back to my West Hampstead flat.

It was an interesting episode and a profitable one. I never received the final five thousand on each book deal of course but the thirty thousand I'd already been given was still good money for a 'yesterday's man' writer. My days of finding favour in the eyes of television script editors may be long past, but working in that medium teaches you a lot of useful stuff. For instance you learn that in the shires of fictional England, it is never a good idea to go into the woods on your own at night. The other thing you learn is that, no matter how vivid your imagination, real life will always be stranger than fiction.

I was very aware that Jeremy still had friends so I

sorted out my life in the UK as fast as I could then returned to New York. My new agent cut a good deal for me to combine my two draft books into one volume, telling the story of the Sinfield brothers from their different points of view in alternate chapters. There's even talk of a film next year.

My wife left me long ago, just as Jeremy's did, but unlike Jeremy I don't mind, at least not now. It's easier to keep secrets when you live alone. A secret shared is not a secret at all.

And these days I can afford to buy my own bottle of Talisker, a beautiful single malt whisky from the Isle of Skye, whisky I was first introduced to on the Isle of Dogs when two manipulative men equated being broke with being gullible and so underestimated the imagination of a writer.

POSTCARDS FROM PARIS

Île de la Cité

She stood on the Pont Neuf gazing down on the Seine, her hand resting lightly on the stone balustrade warm from the sun. This was one of her favourite spots in Paris. Behind her the muddy waters of the river split and swirled either side of the Île de la Cité. Below, she could see the Place Dauphine and the Quai des Orfèvres. She could almost see Inspector Maigret coming out of his office and heading for the Brasserie Dauphine for his midday pastis. Around her was the roar of the traffic – traffic which seemed to have a special sound of its very own. She lifted her head to inhale the aroma of this city, her city. She closed her eyes. She was happy.

I couldn't decide if I was like angry or miserable or unbelieving or outraged. One thing was certain though. I was not happy.

My dad often says that so-and-so couldn't organise a piss-up in a brewery and I've never really understood that till now. I mean, how can you screw up a simple thing like an ID card? Especially if you're a teacher.

And it's the one absolutely can't-do-without thing for a school trip.

I just stood there. In the school hall. With Katy and the others all round me clutching their bits of cardboard hearing Miss Tomlinson say: "I'm sorry, Clare, I don't understand it, but you're not on the ID card list."

"Of course I'm on the bloody list," I said, anger and disappointment and frustration getting the better of common sense. "My Dad paid the money and everything."

"Yes, I know," says Miss Tomlinson, either oblivious or choosing not to hear the particular adjective I'd used. "You're on the list for the trip and on the list for having paid, but you're not on the ID card list and there isn't one for you."

I clung to what seemed to me to be the important thing. "But if I've paid I can still go, can't I?"

"Well, no, I'm so sorry, Clare. I don't know how this has happened but there's no ID card so you're not on the school passport which means, oh, this is terrible, it means you can't go."

Bloody end of the world. End of all life. End of civilisation as we know it. How can this happen? How can bloody adults let it happen?

"Well, can't you get me on this passport thing? I've paid the money."

"I'm sorry, Clare," she says again, "I would if I could, but it's Friday afternoon and we leave on Sunday. There's nothing we can do. We'll obviously give you your money back but ..."

Anger and embarrassment now. There's me surrounded by all the others, all the others who are going to Paris on Sunday, trying to look sympathetic but deep down really enjoying it all. Even Katy – Katy who wasn't really interested in going to Paris in the first place and just wanted a few days off school.

"It's a real shame, Clare," she says in that squeaky little high voice she uses when she is trying to show some kind of emotion. "I know how much you wanted to go to Paris."

"No, you don't," I thought, "you have no idea. I don't just want to go to Paris, I have a passion about Paris. I have lived and dreamed Paris ever since the trip was announced. And now these stupid bloody teachers have stuffed me."

I didn't say that last bit out loud, of course. I'd already realised I'd been pretty lucky to get away with my choice of vocabulary once with Miss Tomlinson. No point in pushing my luck.

"I'll bring you back a present," says Katy and some of the others nod and smile as if a present will make up for the pain of no Paris. Gradually they all drift away to start their packing and count their Euros and

I'm left alone with Miss Tomlinson.

You could tell she was embarrassed and, I suppose to be fair, she was upset for me. But it didn't help. She edged away muttering something about phoning my parents to explain and arrange for a refund but I just stood there. It was like the sun had gone in and wouldn't be coming out again. It might shine down on Paris next week but I wouldn't be there to see it. No Arc de Triomphe, no Eiffel Tower, no Notre-Dame. I'd be stuck in Byfleet doing my bloody homework.

And that was Friday.

The air in the Jardin du Luxembourg smelled fresh and sweet in spite of the taxis and trucks snarling around its circumference. She sat on a chair in the sun, looking across the lake where the ducks squabbled and dived. She watched the students from the nearby Sorbonne, walking alone or hand in hand or studying or kissing and she felt the impossible urge to be young again. Young in years but with the experience of age. On the far side of the lake she could see the Palais du Luxembourg, its windows throwing back the reflection of the sun. She was warm. She was relaxed. Paris, her Paris, flowed around her. She was happy.

Saturday was a funny sort of day. Katy phoned up after breakfast but I told Mum I didn't want to speak to her. Nothing to say. She was going to Paris and I wasn't. Maybe she was like feeling guilty. Her problem.

I know I don't often say it, but Mum and Dad were great. Showed just enough anger with the school so I knew they were on my side and then let it go. Best thing really. There was nothing they could do and deep down I knew that, given any encouragement, I would've had a good mope. I've done that before and there's a kind of like gloomy satisfaction about it, but it doesn't get you anywhere.

I decided to go into Woking and get a couple of new tops – retail therapy Mum calls it. As I was going out the door Dad gave me a wink and twenty quid and said, "Get yourself something nice, darling." Almost made me cry so I gave him a quick hug and went off to catch the bus.

Didn't seem such a good idea when I got into the Peacocks shopping centre. Everyone was bustling about, cheerful, all having a good time. All I could think of was that I wasn't going to Paris, so I slumped down onto one of the benches and tried to have a surreptitious cry. I don't have a problem about crying, but it isn't easy trying to have a good cry without anyone noticing, so I was really gutted when this old bat festooned in shawls and shopping bags plonked herself down right beside me.

Great, I thought, *all I need now is some old dosser trying to cadge the price of a bottle of cider off me.*

Then I recognised her. Lives round the corner from us. Foreign. Weird. Talks to herself. Probably got a thousand cats or something in her kitchen. She was looking straight at me so I kind of gave her a half smile and started getting ready to get up and go when suddenly she says, "Why are you sad?" in a sort of foreign, slurry way.

Great, I thought, *if I wanted to pour my heart out it wouldn't be to this old freak.* But she's harmless, she doesn't smell like so many old people do and at least she's trying to like be kind." So I give her my brave smile and say, "Oh, I've had a bit of a disappointment, that's all."

"Ah, oui, zat is sad," she says and suddenly, dunno why, I'm telling her all about it. And she listens too. Not all adults do that even if they pretend to. And the funny thing is, I think she really does understand.

Then right out of the blue she says, "Paree. Ah, Paree is my town. It is verry sad you cannot go."

"Your town," I say, "what do you mean, your town? You don't live there, do you?"

"Not now," she says and for a moment I think she is going to cry too. Then she sort of pulls herself together and leans forward.

"Do you know, Paree?" she asks, "you 'ave been

210

zere, yes?"

"No," I say, "that's the point. I haven't. I've always wanted to go, and I thought I was going to, but now I'm not."

"Merde," she says, which I think is rude in French. "Zis not good."

Too right it isn't, I thought, *but why are you getting so worked up?*

Then – and this is the really odd bit – she leans forward very close to me, bit too close really, and says, "But you shall go to Paree. I, Cherie, will take you."

Oh, right, I think, *Cinderella you shall go to the ball. So where are the pumpkins and the rats?*

Then she grins and suddenly I think I could like this lady.

"I know what is in your 'ead," she says. "You zink I am, 'ow you say, bonkers, yes?"

I find myself grinning back. "Yeah, a bit."

"I am not bonkers and we cannot go to ze real Paree but I can take you zere in your mind."

"Hang on a minute, I'm not doing any hypnotism or any stuff like that."

"Non, non." she waves a dismissive hand and all the shawls shake. "Non, you come to my 'ome and I will show you my Paree, my pictures, my cartes postales, all my lovely zings and it will be as if you are in Paree yourself."

Says you, I thought to myself, but I was a bit intrigued.

"You come tomorrow. You know where I live, yes?"

"Yes, in that big house in Sycamore Road, opposite the phone box."

"Zat is correct. You come zere tomorrow. À midi. Tu comprends?"

"Yeah, at midday; but I don't know ..."

"Please to come. You would not let Cherie down? You can spare a leetle time for an old woman, yes?"

"Well, if you put it like that..."

"C'est bon. Jusqu'à demain. À midi. Au revoir." And she gathers her shawls about her and disappears into the crowds.

Weird. And yet ... I dunno... sort of nice.

And that was Saturday.

A thin sun sprinkled the view of Paris as she gazed out across the city from the terrace. Everything seemed slightly out of focus, soft edged buildings, splashes of light, faded colour. She knew the reality was a living city, dirty, noisy, busy, impersonal, but seen in this light from up here it was more like a Monet painting. Behind her were the fairy-tale domes of Sacré-Coeur. In the distance she could see the twin towers of Notre-Dame thrusting up into the sky from the Île de la Cité. Below her were the long flights of steps which had brought her up from La Place Saint-Pierre – she was still a little breathless from the climb. Sacré-Coeur. The highest spot in Paris. The cries of the children on the merry-go-round on the terrace below seemed to come from a long way off. The buzz of the crowds was muted. There was just her, the postcard picture building and the view across Paris. Her Paris. Her City. She sighed in pleasure as she gazed out across the rooftops. She was happy.

Right up to the last minute I wasn't sure I'd go, but it was Sunday. They'd be arriving at the school now, getting on the coach to take them to Folkestone, through the tunnel, across France to … Paris. I couldn't bear thinking about that. I had to do something, so I went.

The first surprise was Cherie's house. It was all hers. I suppose I'd always thought she just had a room there or something. I mean, you know, like she didn't dress or behave like a lady who owned a house with 3 floors. Okay, I admit it, I always thought she was a bit of a tramp. But that house. It was something else. The furniture. The pictures. The ornaments and stuff. I'm not normally one for fancy nick-knacks. 'Dust gatherers' Mum calls them, and I'm always afraid I'm going to send them flying but here, I dunno, they just kind of seemed right.

So anyway, she lets me in. Seems really pleased to see me which was sort of nice. She's dressed in this, well, I suppose you'd call it a gown. It was long and flowing, brushing the floor as she walked and when she turned round to lead me into the house I could see it didn't have much back. Yeah, yeah, I know. The thought that this wasn't quite above board passed through my mind too but it didn't feel like that.

Anyway, Cherie takes me up the stairs to this kind of living room on the first floor. She called it her salon. I'm more used to sitting rooms downstairs and bedrooms upstairs but it was kind of nice, sitting there in this kind of rigid upright armchair – don't know how else to describe it – looking down on the street below. Different.

It was an old fashioned sort of room really but it felt right. I mean, you know how it is, some people buy furniture and stuff 'cos they like it, never mind if it fits with stuff they've already got. I mean Katy's mum has these deep red armchairs with bright yellow curtains. It's horrible.

Cherie's stuff is all old looking but sort of fits together. Feels okay. Bit like doing a drawing in art when Mr Bates says you've got all the bits right but they don't hang together and make a picture. "Bit of a pig's breakfast" is one of his favourite phrases.

Katy's sitting room is a bit of a pig's breakfast if

you ask me but Cherie's salon is … Well, a bit like a painting really. But a painting you could live in, if you see what I mean.

She puts this record on and I mean a record, not a CD. The record deck looks as if it ought to have one of those big horns, you know with the dog staring into it.

"Do you know ze music of Jacques Ibert?" she asks, and I don't, of course, but somehow feel I should.

"Well …" I say cautiously, but she goes on, "Zis piece is called *Divertisement* and for me it captures ze spirit of Paree."

We listen to it for a few moments and then she asks me why I wanted to go to Paris and I don't know what to say. I like French, I like the sound of the language, though I'm not very good at it. Not yet. But I will be. I am determined to be. I try and explain but it's not easy. We've never had foreign holidays, not like a lot of the girls at school. Well, it's been difficult with Dad's redundancy and everything. I don't mind. Don't like lying on beaches in the sun anyway, but something about Paris captured my heart.

I've never said this to anyone before – they'd probably just laugh – but my heart aches for Paris. I know it's just another city but to be somewhere like that, café terraces, people talking French all round you, drinking wine, the shutters on the windows, oh, I don't know. I just want it so. And I thought I'd got it and then … then …

To my embarrassment I find I am crying, really crying this time and I feel such an idiot but then Cherie is beside me, her arm is round my shoulders, no, not like that, more like Mum, only foreign, and she's saying: "Do not cry, cherie, be calm …" and for a moment I think she is talking to herself before I realise what she means.

Then she stands up and announces: "It is aperitif time. We will 'ave a drink". A pause and then she says: "'Ow old are you, Clare?"

"Fifteen," I say through my sniffles.

"Ah, quinze ans. Zen we will put a drop of water in your wine, n'est-ce pas?"

"It's all right," I say, "we have wine at home. Sometimes. Well, occasionally."

"Non. Wine is good. Too much strong wine is not."

She goes out of the room while I try and repair some of the damage to my eyes with a rather ancient tissue with Jacques Ibert roaring away in the background.

Cherie comes back with two wine glasses, well, they're more like goblets really, and a bottle of red wine. She makes me sit on an upright chair at a small table: "Like a café terrace, non?" Then she becomes the waiter: "Une verre de vin pour Madame et Madmoiselle, oui?"

She produces a corkscrew, opens the bottle and pours two glasses, then she adds some water from a small odd shaped bottle to one of the glasses. "Voilà, madame."

She sits down beside me and speaks to the non-existent waiter. "Merci, monsieur. Et le menu aussi, s'il vous plait."

"Certainment, madame."

Cherie lifts her glass and turns to me. "I drink ze toast to Clare, to 'er first visit to my Paree."

I accept all this as though it's real. And somehow it is. I drink. The wine, even with a touch of water, is warm and, I don't know, sort of round. I take another gulp.

"Doucement, cherie," says Cherie. "Do not attack your wine, savour it, enjoy its taste in ze mouth. Let it linger."

I try again more slowly and she's right. It does linger. It seems to have two flavours, the first when you taste it and the second a few moments later when you swallow.

So I sit there savouring red wine, gazing down at the street below while Cherie tells me of Paris, her Paris. She describes the streets, the boulevards, the restaurants, the markets, the café terraces, the hooting of the taxis, the architecture. She talks about the way French women dress. She goes away and comes back with armfuls of clothes, clothes of a kind I have never seen before. We both try some on and it is still perfectly innocent. Innocent and beautiful.

Later she produces French bread and a rather runny cheese. She puts out little dishes of chopped raw vegetables which she says are crudies ... or something like that. Crude they might be, but they taste wonderful. She talks about Molière and Debussy, Gaugin and Mallarmé. She rummages in a drawer and pulls out a box of postcards, all of Paris, some of the city today, some of Paris before the war and in the 1950s.

She shows me a picture of Notre-Dame and describes how you walk along the banks of the Seine and over the Pont de l'Archevêché: "Ze most narrow bridge in Paree ..." onto the Île de la Cité – "Ze 'eart of Paris, Clare." And you walk past Notre-Dame along Le Quai des Orfèvres, past La Palais de Justice and up onto the Pont Neuf.

She produces a big book full of colour pictures of paintings, paintings which Cherie says are all hanging in the Louvre. Mr Bates has talked about some of these in his art class but I never paid much attention. Now though, thinking of them in Paris, they become much more interesting. I don't really know any of the artists or recognise the paintings, apart from the Mona Lisa which makes Cherie smile.

"Everyone knows zis picture, yes? It is one of ze most famous in ze world."

She talks about the Louvre, waving her arms around so wildly that I surreptitiously move my wine glass out of the danger zone. She talks about how it was built as a fortress, became a palace and eventually the home of so much art, antique furniture and the like. As she talks I can see the high vaulted rooms, smell the individual aroma of the furniture, visualise the old paintings in their elaborate frames, struggle with the crowd around the Mona Lisa, the magnet in the building.

The Jacques Ibert ended long ago and now Cherie leaps at her record deck and I hear Debussy, Francoise Hardy, Stephane Grappelli and Edith Piaff in rapid succession.

I know none of them, except I seem to recognise the name of Piaff, and when her deep, gravelly voice announces: "Je ne regrette rien …" something turns over in my stomach.

Cherie takes my hand and we move through the house together. There are Toulouse-Lautrec posters on the wall and suddenly we are in Montmartre – night clubs, smoky bars with a chanteuse, barmen in white shirts and black aprons – and then suddenly, there in front of us is the Moulin Rouge.

This is familiar. I've seen the film ... several times ... well, six times actually as I really fancy Ewan McGregor. I start humming the music of '*The Show Must Go On*' as we make our way back to her salon but then, without any warning, the mood changes.

Cherie stops and suddenly, although she is standing in front of me, I know she's not with me anymore but somewhere far, far away. I go to speak but there's something in her eyes that stops me. Instead, I take her hand and gently lead her back to her salon, almost as though I was taking a child across the road.

Once safely back in her chair she shakes her head and is with me again.

"Are you all right?" I ask. To be honest I'm a bit worried in case she's having some kind of turn like Granny did that day at Bognor.

"Is nothing," says Cherie, "I am sorry, ma chère. It is just zat film. I remember ze way it begins and ... it ... it touches me."

I concentrate, trying to remember the opening of the film. "Do you mean the song '*Nature Boy*'?"

And Cherie nods. "Ze words of zat song, Clare, zey are telling of a strange, enchanted boy. A boy who wandered very far only to learn that the greatest thing … was just to love and be loved in return. Zat is perhaps the most important lesson of all."

I think about this. To be honest I'd never really considered it before. It was just part of the moody opening before we're thrust into the excitement, noise and colour of the Moulin Rouge. To love and be loved. In spite of myself I shiver and suddenly I have a fleeting glimpse of the future and I sense this is a moment to be treasured.

I glance at Cherie and see that her face has turned inward again. She looks sad and lost and I want to cheer her up.

"Come on," I say, jumping up. "Let's have some more music."

I grab the first record that comes to hand and, slightly clumsily, manage to get the needle somewhere onto the surface at random and suddenly the room is filled with this haunting piano music. I am entranced. I have never heard anything like it.

Cherie stirs and her face loses that sad inward expression and she smiles, a real smile that reaches her eyes.

"Ah, Erik Satie," she says, "Gymnopédies. Zere is nothing quite like it, non?"

She gets to her feet and suddenly we are busy, busy, busy again. More clothes, this time including hats, all of which look silly on me but make us both laugh. More books, architecture this time and a series of photographs of the Seine through the ages, all black and white.

"All ze best photos of Paree are in black and white," says Cherie, "zey give you ze picture, you add your own colour, yes?"

We have another drink, Cherie summons the non-existent waiter and orders an omelette aux fine herbes for two – which she actually goes and cooks herself. It is delicious.

And suddenly it is time to go. I try to thank her. She doesn't let me.

"Zank you for coming," she says, "zank you for letting me share my Paree with someone who cares."

"May I come again sometime?"

"Mais certainement. It will be a pleasure."

I turn to go but she stops me with a quick gesture. "Un moment."

She goes into her bedroom and comes out a moment later with a carrier bag which she hands to me. I peer inside and see a small oblong parcel wrapped in coloured paper.

"Un cadeau. A small gift. I want you to 'ave this for sparing time for a bonkers old lady." The expression on her face seems to be both warm and sad at the same time.

"You're not bonkers," I say and then, "thank you.

222

That's very kind. Shall I …"

"Non, non, do not open it now. Save it until
tomorrow. Today you are 'appy. Tomorrow you may
be sad again, zinking of your friends. Open it zen. It
may 'elp."

She leans forward and kisses me on both cheeks
and then the door closes behind me.

Walking home, my head filled with images of
Paris and life on the boulevards, I was surprised at
how happy I felt. Katy and the others would be in
Paris by now, checking in to their hotel, sticking
their toothbrushes in plastic tumblers, but I had been
taken to the heart of the real Paris or so it seemed to
me. One day I would go there for real, but I already
felt as though I knew the city, had tasted its flavours,
seen into its heart.

When I got home Dad was in the living room.
"Had a good day, love? How was your old lady?"

"Oh, Dad, she was so cool. It was wonderful. She
gave me some wine, oh, not very much, and some
food and stuff and we talked about Paris, the real
Paris, her Paris. Oh, Dad, she does love that city but
I get the feeling she's pretty lonely."

"Yes, she is. Not surprising really. Did she tell you
anything about herself?"

I thought for a moment. "No, not really. It was all
about Paris not about her."

My father nodded. "I'm not surprised, though I am rather surprised you got invited there. Not many people go into that house."

"Why not?"

"Well, as you know, I've lived here since I was a boy and that lady has always been something of a recluse. She must have lived alone in that house now for over 40 years. Her husband was killed, you know, sometime in the 1960s. He worked for one of the French banks, I think it was. He was based in London but then they sent him to Algeria, about the time of all the fighting there. He was just in the wrong place at the wrong time."

"Oh, no. Poor Cherie."

"Indeed. Anyway apparently she was pregnant. The shock sent her into early labour and the child was stillborn. The two events coming so close together changed her and she became … well … you know… a lot of people think she's potty."

"I don't think she's potty."

"Maybe not. But she's certainly a little odd."

"What a sad story. But if Cherie was so lonely I wonder why she didn't go back home to Paris."

Dad hesitated for a moment so I knew something difficult was coming.

"Look, Clare, I don't want to spoil your day."

"Tell me."

He sighed. "All right. As far as I know the lady you call Cherie has never been to Paris, in fact I don't think she's ever been abroad. Someone told me they'd planned to move to Paris after the baby was born. Her husband was French but she isn't. Her name is actually Betty Walker."

I sat there, stunned. She had never been to Paris but she knew it, inside out.

"Clare?" Dad was looking anxious now.

I made up my mind. "So, I don't care who she is or where she has been. She gave me a wonderful day. She took me to Paris."

Dad grinned. "Good for you but ..."

"I know. It's not the real thing and one day I'll go there properly but, Dad, honestly, I feel as though I've been there today. She did that for me."

"Good. Will you go and see her again?"

"Yes, and I won't tell her that I know, you know, about her husband and everything."

"Good thinking."

"Dad, do we have any music by Erik Satie?"

And that was Sunday.

She walked slowly through the Tuileries Garden, towards the Louvre, enjoying the green of the grass and the splash of the fountains. This was another favourite walk. By taking the path through the garden from the

Place de la Concorde to the Louvre she could avoid the tourists on the Rue de Rivoli. She must remember to bring Clare here next time they met. She could tell her how today the garden is a place for children to play and for lovers to meet, but those with imagination can still conjure up a vision of the large palace that once stood along the eastern edge. Built by Catherine of Medici, its footprint still defines the shape of the Louvre courtyard. Clare would appreciate that. She gazed round the Tuileries Garden thinking of their next meeting and she was happy.

It was quite difficult waiting until Monday before opening Cherie's present, but I managed it – somehow. The wrapping paper was very thin and had pictures of elegant people in long dresses and what I think must be frock coats walking in a park. You could tell it wasn't English just by looking at it.

I don't know what I was expecting but when I got the paper off and opened the package I just sat there, stunned. Inside, nestling on a bed of cotton wool was a beautiful little box and on its lid was Notre-Dame sort of raised up so you could feel the edges. I lifted the box out very carefully and set it down on the table. It sort of sparkled in the light. Then I lifted the lid and at once it began to play *'I Love Paris in the Springtime'*.

"It's a musical jewel box," said Mum when I showed her. "You're meant to keep your rings in it. I think it must be quite old. Are you sure she meant you to have it?"

I remembered the look on Cherie's face when she gave me the present. "Yes," I said, "I'm sure she did."

"Well, you must write and thank her," said Mum, "it's a beautiful gift."

She stood in the courtyard outside Notre-Dame on the Île de la Cité, oblivious of the crowds around her. In front of her, the twin towers of the gothic cathedral reached for the sky, the famous flying buttresses not visible from this side. She had no strong views about religion – to her the building was a symbol of her Paris. She imagined she could elevate herself high above the city to look down on the courtyard, to see the cathedral complete, in all its architectural glory, standing at the end of the Île de la Cité, the Seine flowing past on both sides. She had been here many times before but now she had shown it to Clare she realised what pleasure there was in sharing. She looked forward to their next visit here together, to Paris. Her Paris. She had always been happy here but now she realised she was full of joy.

Three days later the school trip arrived home. The coach was meant to get back to the school at about six but there had been some kind of security alert in the Channel Tunnel so they had to come back by ferry instead. It was nearly nine before they actually arrived. I thought I'd go and meet them, so after tea I walked down to the school and waited there with all the parents and teachers.

When the coach finally stopped outside the school, everyone on board looked a bit tired and irritable. There had been a strong wind in the Channel and it had been a rough crossing and several of the group were not feeling at all well.

Katy had not been ill, but she was not in the best of moods.

"How was it?" I asked.

"Sort of all right. Rained most of the time and I don't care if I never seen another museum as long as I live. Anyway, I got you this," and she thrust a small bag into my hand. I opened it and found a plastic pencil sharpener in the shape of Notre-Dame, each of the twin towers offering accommodation for a different sized pencil.

"Thanks," I said.

"Sorry you couldn't come but you didn't miss much. Pretty boring really, Paris. Just another town with lots of traffic."

For a moment I was tempted, but Katy was tired and it seemed unkind to tell her what I'd been doing.

It would keep. Katy had her Paris, I had mine. I don't know how Katy felt, but I was happy.

NOTHING TO FEAR

The Islets of Langerhans

The day Beth Radcliffe learned she was going to die it was raining. She didn't mind that, she had always liked the feel of gentle rain on her face, but she did resent dying. Although she would admit to being 78, she wasn't ready to call it a day. There were still many things she wanted to do. Bit like being ordered out of the theatre in the interval, she thought, and she felt quite malevolent towards the tiny little growth that had sneaked in to upset all her plans.

She had intended to treat herself to a taxi back to the city centre but she decided she needed some time – some slow time – to mull over what the consultant had said. So she caught a bus to the ring road and then walked. It took her a long time, but she didn't rush. There was a lot to think about and somehow the overcast day with light rain falling made the situation easier to face.

In a way, it was fortunate that Edward had died two years ago. She could just imagine how he would have worried about her, cosseted her, made her sit down all the time, brought her cups of tea as though tea could deal with this. Dear Edward. He was always so kind, so solicitous and so very, very impractical. Although he would have done his best, she would have ended up having to worry about him.

By the time she was walking down Castle Hill her legs were getting tired so on the spur of the moment she went into the museum café and, with an inward nod to Edward, ordered a pot of tea. She was tempted by their scones but decided that would be indulgent, then changed her mind and ordered them after all. The tea was hot and strong, and as she felt the warmth of it flowing through her, she began to feel more positive. She quite deliberately didn't think about the decision she had to face. She wanted to let things settle in her mind, think round the question for a while. She had never been one to make hurried decisions and she was not going to start now.

The speed of the whole sequence of events was still rather a shock. It was barely three months since she first acknowledged to herself that something wasn't quite right. She was sweating more than usual, seemed to have acquired a voracious appetite and she had started to realise that the occasional dizzy spell was not entirely attributable to her homemade elderflower wine.

Beth had never been sensitive about her health, unlike Edward who at the first sign of a sniffle had retired to bed and looked at her with sad eyes when she asked if he wanted anything. She had always accepted that advancing age brought certain inevitable consequences. When friends asked how she was, she ignored such things as the pain from the arthritis in her finger joints, the stiffness in her knees when she had been weeding, taking these as the inevitable base line.

She thought that perhaps she'd been overdoing things and had tried to slow down a bit, but then one day, just as she was setting out to go shopping, she found herself falling. She must have passed out for a few minutes for when she came round, she was lying on the doormat with her shopping basket a few feet away.

After that she knew she had no choice and made an appointment at the surgery for the next day. The doctor she saw – yet another locum and young enough to be her grandson – examined her carefully, asked a number of questions but was non-committal when she asked him what was wrong. When she pushed him, he said he wasn't sure and there was probably nothing to worry about but he would be happier if she went to the hospital for a few tests.

That 'probably' worried her quite a lot, a worry

that was not lessened when she was given a hospital appointment within a week. Speed in the health service, she had always thought, meant bad news.

The consultant she saw was a bit more forthcoming. "We need to do a few more tests, Mrs Radcliffe," he said, "but it looks as though your body may be producing excess insulin."

"Excess insulin? Does that mean I have diabetes?"

"No, not exactly, though we may need to discuss diet as part of the treatment."

She managed a smile. "Eat, drink and be merry, for tomorrow we diet."

He looked at her for a moment, then smiled. "Very good. Are you on a diet at the moment, by any chance?"

"Me? No, I don't need to. Anyway, I always seem to be hungry these days."

He nodded. "Okay, we'll see how it goes. Now then, you need to make another appointment."

She soon became quite used to the journey. She had given up driving some years earlier and it took two buses to get her to the hospital, but she had her bus pass and was in no great hurry. There were several neighbours or friends who would have given her a lift if she'd asked but something made her keep this situation to herself. She told no-one where she was going and told no-one of her fears.

Eventually the process was completed and she went to see the consultant for his verdict. They sat in his room and he briefly summarised the various tests they had done, until she could wait no longer.

"I know what you've done. I was there. It was me you did it to. Now can you please tell me what's wrong with me."

He nodded. "Of course. I'm sorry. I didn't mean to prevaricate. I don't think there is any doubt, Mrs Radcliffe. You have a condition we call an insulinoma."

"That's this excess of insulin you were talking about?"

"Yes, but it's not quite as simple as that. What has happened is that something called the Islets of Langerhans ..."

"Oh, I know about those," she interrupted, "They're a favourite trick question in quizzes, aren't they? *Where are the Islets of Langerhans?* Most people say in the Indian Ocean but they're not actually islands at all, they're something in the kidneys, aren't they?"

The consultant smiled. "Close. They're in the pancreas and in simple terms they're the regulators which control the level of blood sugar."

"So it is diabetes."

"No. What can happen – well, what has happened

in your case – is that sometimes there's an excessive growth of the islets inside the pancreas which can cause problems."

"What sort of problems?"

"Well, to put it simply they get over-excited about producing insulin and churn out a lot of it, more than is actually needed."

"I see. And this is a kind of growth, is it?"

"Yes, and it's usually benign but …"

"Sometimes it isn't?"

"Yes, sometimes it isn't."

"And what is mine?"

"We don't know, not for certain. My instinct is that it's benign but looking at the scan, the lump that's secreting the insulin has a rather unusual shape so we would like to take some cells and look at them under a microscope to make sure."

"I see. I presume this means you're going to want to open me up and chop a bit out?"

The consultant winced. "Well, in principle, yes, though 'open up' is a little dramatic and we certainly won't be doing any chopping. It's quite a simple procedure. We give you a local anaesthetic, then pop you into a CT scanner so we can see what's going on."

"And how do you get the cells you need?"

"Long needle, guided by what we see on the scan.

You really won't feel a thing."

"Won't I?" She thought for a moment. "When do you want to do this?"

"The sooner, the better. I'd certainly like to get it done in the next week or so. I also think it best, forgive me, given your age, if we keep you in for a couple of days so we can keep an eye on you."

In the event she had to wait ten days. The waiting was not easy. She wasn't frightened by the idea of a biopsy but she wasn't looking forward to it either. The thought of lying in a scanner while they stuck a needle into her innards was a little disconcerting, but the logical side of her mind told her this was clearly a common and safe procedure and all she had to do was to be a sensible patient.

On the day itself, as she had expected, Logic and Emotion fought a silent battle inside her head but she managed to summon up reinforcements on behalf of Logic and told Emotion, politely but firmly, to go away. After that everything passed without incident and, as promised, she didn't feel a thing.

Then, two weeks later, came the moment of truth back in the consultant's office with the results of the biopsy no doubt lying in that folder in front of him.

She knew it wasn't straightforward the moment he said "Good morning" and briefly she felt as though her heart had stopped. Then instantly she regained control, moved forward, sat down and looked him straight in the eye.

"It's bad news, isn't it?"

He met her gaze and she was grateful that she had found an honest man. She knew he wouldn't lie to her or offer false comfort.

"It's not the news we wanted I'm afraid. There's a localised area of growth as I expected but it seems it's not benign."

"I see." There was a pause as she considered what questions she needed to ask. The consultant said nothing but did not look down and she took strength from him.

After a moment she said. "What happens now?"

"We have two choices. Either we operate to try and remove this growth or we see if it will respond to a non-invasive treatment."

"And in order to remove it you really would have to open me up?"

A faint smile touched his lips. "Yes, but I can assure you we won't be doing anything as crude as 'chopping'."

She returned his smile. "No, I don't suppose you will."

There was a short silence. Then she said. "And this non-invasive treatment? What's that?"

"Basically medication, coupled with a controlled

diet. We will also have to consider chemotherapy."

"Which option would you recommend?"

"Surgery would be my preferred choice. It stands more chance of success, though it's not without risks. There is also a reasonable expectation that we won't need to follow it with chemotherapy. We can discuss the details of both routes in more depth of course."

There was another pause, then she said. "I don't like the sound of chemotherapy. On the other hand, surgery at my age is not an attractive prospect either. What happens if we do nothing?"

She had been right in her assessment of the man. Very gently he said, "If we do nothing then you will die."

She nodded. "I thought so. How quickly?"

"Impossible to be precise but I would say sooner rather than later."

She nodded again. "Just now, when you first mentioned surgery, you said you would try and remove this growth. The word 'try' suggests that you might not succeed."

There was a short silence. Then he said. "No, we might not succeed. It depends on a number of things, such as how localised it is, and we won't really know until we explore further."

A sense of mischief rose up in her. "Suppose I were a horse running in the Grand National. What odds would you give me that I will make it to the finishing post? I don't have to win the race, you understand, just finish it."

For the first time since she had entered the room he looked a bit startled. "A horse?"

She made an impatient gesture. "What are the odds on my coming through an operation?"

He took a deep breath. "I'm very sorry, Mrs Radcliffe. I think you are a very brave and intelligent woman, and we will of course go through all the possible complications in more detail, but I'm sure you'll understand when I say, I don't do percentages."

"No, no, of course not. I'm sorry."

"Please don't apologise. This is obviously a shock."

"Yes, it is rather." There was a long silence as Beth, in her normal organised way, assembled a mental tick list of all the options. The consultant sat silently waiting for her to speak but his eyes never left her face.

Finally, she nodded to herself as though confirming a decision. "I think I understand all the implications. Doing nothing is not an option. After that it comes down to a choice between surgery, which could be kill or cure," – The consultant winced again – "Or you experiment with various forms of medication, which could include chemotherapy, to see if you can find something that works for me. Is that a fair summary?"

"More or less."

"And when do I need to decide?"

"I'd quite like you to do that now."

Beth shook her head decisively. "No. There's a lot to think about. I need some time."

"I understand. Then I suggest we meet again a week from now, next Wednesday suit you?" She nodded. "Good. I'll see you then and whatever your decision we'll put matters in hand."

"You said we could discuss the options in more detail. Can we do that now?"

"Of course we can." He hesitated. "I can't tell you how sorry I am about this, Mrs Radcliffe. I appreciate it's no help to you but it's very rare for growths like this not to be benign."

Beth thought about that remark as she went to the museum café for another cup of tea. The consultant was right, of course, it was no help at all to realise that she was an unusual statistic, but she didn't feel hard done by either. She had always seen life as a series of random events, some good, some bad, some neutral. It was all chance and you simply had to deal with things as best you could as they came up. All the same it was a nuisance. She sighed, paid her bill, gathered up her handbag and went off to catch the bus home.

She lit the fire when she got in and, as usual, the light of the flames reflecting off the cottage walls cheered her. Beth was not a natural pessimist, her glass was usually half full, but she was also realistic and would not indulge herself with false hope. Neither of the options before her were pleasant but all the same she had to choose. She had seven days. She rather felt they were going to be long days.

In the meantime, there was something she had to do at once. It was time to tell her daughter what was going on. She didn't really want to share this with anyone but she was very close to Deborah and her husband, Richard. It was unfortunate they lived so far away but she felt Deborah had a right to know what was happening. She poured another cup of tea and picked up the phone.

Thursday. The following morning about ten there was a knock at the door and it was Marjorie looking suspiciously bright and cheerful. Marjorie and Frank from the converted barn up the hill had always been close friends but random visits were rare, so when Marjorie smiled brightly and said, "Just thought I'd pop in for a quick cuppa and see how you're doing…" Beth had to fight back a smile.

"Come in," she said, "lovely to see you. I'll put the kettle on."

They talked of this and that while she made the tea and cut a couple of slices of cake then, when they had sat down, Beth said: "Did you have a nice chat with Deborah?"

"Well, I don't know if you'd call it nice ..." Marjorie began and then blushed. "How did you know I'd been talking to Deborah?"

Beth laughed. "Oh, come on, Marjorie. I had a long, meaningful conversation with my daughter on the phone last night and then you pop up on the doorstep bright as a button this morning. It's not exactly a Sherlock Holmes challenge, is it?"

"Don't be unkind, Beth. Deborah's worried about you and so am I. She can't get over here quickly but I'm just round the corner so she rang me."

"She doesn't have to get over here at all, quickly or otherwise. I told her, there's nothing she can do."

"Well, she's going to come anyway. Just as soon as she's sorted things out."

Beth sighed. "Yes, I suppose she will. Can't trust Mum to make up her own mind."

"She's worried about you and wants to help," said Marjorie, "though I'm still not sure what the problem is. Deborah said you were going into hospital but wasn't very clear about why."

"I don't know if I am going into hospital yet. I haven't decided."

"Oh? I thought … well, Deborah said you had to have an operation?"

"That's what Deborah thinks I should do but there are other options. I have to decide what's best for me."

Marjorie put down her cup. "Why not tell me exactly what's happened, from the beginning."

"To be honest, Marjorie, I don't really want to talk about it yet. I've got a lot of thinking to do."

"You're starting to frighten me, Beth. What exactly is wrong? Please tell me. I might be able to help."

"You can't, but thank you."

"It's no good keeping it to yourself. You'll only fret."

"I don't fret", Beth thought, "you're the one who frets, Marjorie". But she appreciated the concern that was being expressed, so reluctantly she said. "It's to do with my blood sugar levels. They're not under control."

Marjorie gave a huge sigh of relief. "Oh, you mean you've got diabetes. Oh, that's all right. Lots of people have that. It just means a careful diet and eating regularly and all that stuff. Oh, Beth, you had me worried there for a minute."

"Well, it's not actually diabetes, not as such." She realised that having started she had to finish so she went on. "It's actually something called an insulinoma. I've got an excessive growth of these things – the Islets of Langerhans and basically they're not doing what they're meant to do, or rather, they're doing rather too much of what they're meant to do and that's not good either."

"Oh … Right …" said Marjorie looking puzzled, "but is it serious?"

"Yes."

Marjorie was silent for a minute then she said. "But they can treat it, can't they?"

"Possibly. They could try medication and maybe even a course of chemotherapy or I could have an operation to remove it but that carries its own risks, especially at my age."

"And if it isn't removed?"

"If it isn't removed, then I will be."

"You mean … oh, Beth."

"I need to decide what I'm going to do, but in the meantime …"

"You don't want it spread about, I do understand. I won't tell anyone."

Rather to her surprise Beth found it was something of a relief to have told Marjorie, but of course she should have known. It was impossible to keep secrets in a small village.

Friday. She popped into the village shop for

a pint of milk and as she was coming out old Mr Pullen stopped her and said. "Sorry to hear about the diabetes, Mrs Radcliffe. My mother always recommended a surfeit of raw carrots."

"It's not diabetes," she wanted to say, but old Mr Pullen was as deaf as a post and she didn't feel up to bellowing an explanation about the Islets of Langerhans at full volume down the village street. For the same reason she also felt unable to follow up the fascinating non-sequitur.

Mary Draycott, who was in charge of the flower rota at the church, was gushing. "Oh, you poor love, I'm so sorry. I remember when my sister was diagnosed with that. It was terrible. Up and down like a yoyo she was until they got the balance of the medication right. And then she came out in this awful rash, oh, no, what am I saying. That was the skin rash she got from cutting back her euphorbias without wearing gloves. Her husband, he's the landscape gardener you remember, did warn her, but would she listen. Oh, no – not her …"

Beth, who had never liked Mary Draycott, listened to this verbal diarrhoea with remarkable patience. The woman presumably wanted to be sympathetic, but in her case, it was rather like watching a goldfish trying to play badminton. It did not come naturally.

The postman, who was very efficient and always

very friendly although Beth could never remember his name, was more down to earth.

"Diabetes isn't a problem these days. Don't you worry."

"Well, it isn't actually diabetes. It's an insulinoma, that's an excessive growth of the Islets of Langerhans you see, the things that control the level of blood sugar."

"Sound like diabetes under a fancy name to me. You'll be alright, love, take it from me. Now if you could just sign for this parcel ..." And he was back in his van and away.

In one way the fact that everyone in the village was concerned with the state of her pancreas was rather amusing, but it didn't help her make up her mind about what to do. Sometimes, lying awake in the night, she felt make or break was the answer. Go in, have the operation and hope for the best. If it was successful then problem solved. If it wasn't ... well ... at least it would be a conclusion.

At other times she felt that the operation was too big a gamble. Give the medication a try, she thought, it didn't rule out the idea of surgery later on. But she was very nervous about the thought of chemotherapy, the rigid regime it would involve, potential side effects and after all that – maybe no result.

"I'm too old for all this," she thought. "I was quite

happy pottering along with my ladies' group and the garden. I don't like either of these options but above all I don't like having to decide."

And she was in no doubt that a decision would have to be made. She knew she wasn't right, she'd put on quite a lot of weight quite quickly and the dizzy spells were still occurring. The third option – do nothing – she would not even consider. Beth had never had any patience with passivity. Whatever was going to happen to her had to come about because she had made a positive decision.

Although she was reluctant to talk about her dilemma, the rumours continued to fly round the village, gathering more inaccuracies as they went. On Saturday afternoon in the lane she met the two ladies who shared the ugly bungalow by the bridge. They stopped and patted her on the back.

"Now you're not to worry," said the tall one, "they can do wonders with these obscure blood diseases these days."

"Just let us know if you want any shopping done," squeaked the short one. "Always happy to help a neighbour."

"And the trouble is I know they mean it," she said to her friend Bernard that evening when they were sitting in his conservatory making short work of a decent bottle of Rioja. Bernard Wilshire was a retired banker who lived in the Old Vicarage. She and Edward had been friends with Bernard and Florence for many years, so when first Florence and then Edward had died it seemed natural to get together with Bernard from time to time and share a glass of wine. "If I really were ill, then I know they would help, so would all sorts of people, but I don't want them to, if you see what I mean."

"Do you mean you don't want them to help? Or you don't want to be in a position where you might need that help?"

"I don't know. Well, of course I don't want to be in that position. Oh, this is such a nuisance. I don't even feel ill at the moment." She paused for a moment, remembering the feeling of faintness that had suddenly hit her that morning before breakfast. "Well, not ill-ill. And I'm not sure I like being the talk of the village."

"Small communities. Main interest is your neighbours. No malice in it."

"No, I know, but it is a little disconcerting to have your innards the main subject of conversation wherever you go."

"Have patience. This time next week a cat will get stuck up a tree or the shop will put up a controversial poster. Dogs bark but the caravan moves on."

She sipped her wine. "Bernard ..." she said but he

interrupted her.

"I do hope you're not going to ask me what I think you should do."

"No, I'm not. There's enough people telling me what they think already. None of that helps."

"It wouldn't. It's your decision, Beth. It's pointless any of us saying 'if I were you …' because we're not."

"I'm glad you see that. Deborah doesn't. She thinks I should have the operation. 'Get it cleared up once and for all' as she puts it. Maybe she's right – I appreciate it might be completely successful, but I don't know. There's always a risk of infection and there's no guarantee that these bloody Islet things won't come back, even after the operation. But then I rather dread the chemotherapy route too."

"Rock and a hard place, isn't it?"

"It is rather. Um … Bernard, have you got any more of these biscuit things. I seem to have finished these off."

He went and got another packet and gave her a wry grin. "Is increased appetite one of the symptoms of this Islets thing?"

"Apparently so." She changed the subject quickly. "Marjorie is in the medication camp, but what about the side effects? I want to carry on doing things, not spend my time lying on the sofa looking pale and interesting."

Bernard gave a snort of laughter, splashing some wine down his shirt front in the process. "Must say I can't see you playing the Jane Austen invalid part," he said, "though if it came to it there are plenty of people round here who'd come in and look after you."

"I know there are, and it's nice to know, but I don't want to be looked after."

For a moment she pictured it. Herself, lying languid on the sofa, a tap at the door, a face appearing round the corner, the hushed whisper. "Only me. Just popped in to see if you want anything. I'm going into town later."

A few moments of forced banalities, perhaps asking for a drink of water or a particular book so the visitor felt they'd been useful and then alone again until the next tap and the next peering face.

Oh, no, she couldn't bear it. She gave an involuntary shudder and Bernard asked if she was cold.

"No, not cold, only disgusted with myself." But even Bernard did not understand that.

Sunday – four days to go and she'd still not reached a decision. Marjorie came round in the morning before church suggesting that Beth should go with her for once.

"I know you always say you don't believe …"

"I don't."

"... but just for once. It can't do you any harm and you might be given an inkling of what you should do."

Beth was very firm. "I appreciate your concern, Marjorie, and I value your friendship, but we've never agreed on religion and we won't now. Apart from anything else, don't you think it would be a bit wimpish to deny the existence of something all these years and then change my mind when something goes wrong?"

"But God wouldn't mind, dear. And at least with Him you're never alone."

"We're all alone in the final count, Marjorie. I'm lucky enough to have a lot of friends, especially you, but there are some things no friend can share and this is one of them. I feel loved, cherished and supported, and yet nothing can change the fact that this illness is a very lonely experience. Now, listen, the bells are ending. Hurry up or you'll be late."

So Marjorie, not sure whether to be hurt or flattered, crept away to her hymns and her hope.

Deborah and Richard arrived just before lunch and secretly Beth was very glad to see them. In spite of what she'd said to Bernard, the dizzy spells, especially those first thing in the morning, were beginning to bother her and it felt good not to be alone. Deborah had her own agenda, of course. She was convinced that her mother should have the operation, but she wasn't dogmatic; she simply left Beth in no doubt about what she thought was right.

Richard was more neutral. He took Bernard's line. He made it clear that they would help in any practical way they could, but the actual decision was hers. They told her they'd both taken a few days off work and they planned to stay until after she had seen the consultant again. She tried to be objective about this but found that she was actually grateful not to be alone.

"But I'm still going to make up my own mind, dear," she said to Deborah. "I know what you think I should do but I haven't yet made a decision."

"No, mother," said Deborah in her dutiful daughter voice. Behind her Richard grinned and rolled his eyes upwards.

Monday brought Marjorie again. She greeted Deborah with great enthusiasm. "So good you can be with your mother at this terrible time. Oh, dear what is she going to do? What an awful thing to have happened."

Mother and daughter exchanged glances and together tried to reassure her. Two cups of tea and a slice of cake later Marjorie had calmed down a little and Deborah walked back up the hill with her so that Marjorie could show her what they'd done with the garden since her last visit.

Beth was exhausted. Richard made her sit down and brought her a glass of sherry.

"You're still taking care of everyone in sight, I see," he said.

"Well, you know how it is. People bring you their problems."

"And you take them on board. Don't you think it's time you stopped looking after everyone else and let us look after you."

"You sound like Bernard. I don't want to be looked after."

"I'm sure you don't, but in the circumstances that might be the kindest thing. Take Debbie for instance. She wants to help but deep down she knows there's nothing she can do. Even if it's only making you a cup of tea occasionally, let her do what she can."

Beth was silent for a moment. Then she nodded. "I see what you mean. Trying to cope on my own is rather selfish, isn't it?"

"I wouldn't go that far."

"I take your point, Richard, but the decision about the treatment must be mine and mine alone."

"Of course."

There was a pause and then she said. "To be honest with you, Richard, I'm a bit frightened."

"I know you are." Then he gave her a hug and she

knew he understood.

That afternoon Beth and Deborah went to the supermarket in the nearby town. In the car park they met Mrs Bicknell who flung her arms around Beth, nearly knocking her flying. "Oh, you poor dear, I've just heard. How awful for you. Are you going to have to have one of those stunt things, or whatever they're called, bunged into your arteries?"

Deborah looked stunned and was just about to query this amazing statement when Beth stepped in. "Don't worry, dear, everything's under control. Now, how is Mr Bicknell?"

Immediately the focus shifted. "Oh, not too good, I'm afraid. He's got to go back to the doctor next week. They think they might have to operate."

It was nearly ten minutes before the full extent of Mr Bicknell's problem had been explored and Deborah and Beth made it back to the car. Deborah was livid. "What a stupid woman. She had no idea of what was really wrong with you and all she could do was babble on about her husband's broken toe."

"That's what's important to her," said Beth. "It does no harm to let her talk."

"But what about you, Mother? You're facing more than a broken toe. Do you know what you're going to do yet?"

"Not yet, dear. I'm still thinking."

Tuesday. Tomorrow the final decision would have to be made. Beth suggested to Deborah and Richard that they should go for a long walk before lunch. She stayed at home. She wasn't feeling too good and in any case she wanted some time to herself to think. It was so difficult. It felt like a choice between two evils – actually three evils, because there was always the option of doing nothing. She still hadn't reached any conclusion when Deborah and Richard returned.

The afternoon had one light moment. There was a knock at the door and when Deborah answered it she found old Mother Meg on her doorstep. No-one really knew what her name was. She owned a tiny cottage at the edge of the village but was usually found living in an old caravan in her garden. She was carrying a bunch of nettles roughly tied with a piece of string.

"They tell me you be sick," she began.

"Well, not exactly sick, at least not yet," said Beth.

"Your inner flow is not free," said Meg, "so I was told and now I am here I can feel it. Take these ..." She thrust the nettles at Beth. "Spread them around your room and at midnight touch each one lightly and the blockage will be released."

"I see. Er ... thank you very much."

"You do as I say now. That be fine. Now I must

go, but your choice will be the right one. I discussed it with my goat. All will be well."

Deborah watched her go, open mouthed. "I didn't imagine that, did I? What is she, some kind of witch or something?"

"Of course not, dear. Just an old lady with some very strange ideas."

"What are you going to do with those nettles?"

"Spread them around the room, just as she said. Pretty pointless of course, but she meant well and if she ever asks me if I did it, I don't want to lie. Now then, I presume you will drive me to the hospital in the morning."

"Of course we will. What time do you want to leave?"

"About half past ten should be fine."

"And do you know what you're going to choose?"

Beth hesitated. "No, no I don't."

That night Beth found it hard to sleep. She was sweating badly. She thought of Deborah's certainty and Marjorie's fear. Neither of them were necessarily right. Perhaps there wasn't a 'right' decision, merely the choice of a particular path. Towards dawn she dozed a little, then woke just before seven feeling tired and unrefreshed.

She was very quiet all through breakfast and on the way to the hospital said nothing, just went over the options again and again in her mind. She would not answer Deborah's questions and would not let either of them come up to the clinic with her, asking them to remain downstairs in reception instead.

"I'll come and find you as soon as I'm done," she said. Deborah opened her mouth to speak but Richard put a hand on her arm and she stayed silent. Beth noticed that and appreciated it.

They're a good pair, she thought as she went up in the lift. *They've had their say. I know they'll accept my decision, whatever it is.*

She heard her name called and went into the consultant's office. He came forward, holding out his hand.

"Good morning, Mrs Radcliffe. How are you today?"

"I'm not too bad, thank you."

"Good. And have you made a decision about what you want to do?"

Beth took a deep breath. "Yes, yes I have."

It was a month later when Beth was sitting in the conservatory at Deborah and Richard's house where she had come to convalesce, that Deborah finally asked the question that had been bothering her. Mother and daughter sat side by side looking out over the garden to the sea. Deborah swallowed and then said. "There's something I've been wanting to ask you, Mother."

"What's that, dear?"

"I've been a bit worried. All that time when you didn't know what you were going to do, I may have been ... well ... perhaps a little forceful. I didn't want to bully you. I just wanted ..."

"What was best for me. Of course, you did, Debbie, I understand."

"I've been worried in case you felt ..."

"It made no difference, dear. I made up my own mind."

"But you chose the surgery in the end. Why?"

"Because I was frightened."

"Frightened?"

"Yes. I didn't fancy any of the choices but at the last minute I realised that when it came to surgery, I didn't just dislike the idea, I was actually terrified of it. I wasn't used to being frightened so I decided to face it head on. All right, you nasty little Islets, I thought, you want a fight, you've got one. I'm coming after you."

Deborah burst out laughing. "You're amazing, mother, do you know that."

"Not really, dear, I just couldn't see any point in fooling myself. Didn't someone once say 'There's nothing to fear, but fear itself'? I may or may not have made the right choice. Only time will tell. But it was my choice and I made it. Now, how about a cup of tea?"

ABOUT THE AUTHOR

Michael Bartlett has written for radio and television for over 40 years. He has been a regular writer for hit programmes such as *The Archers* (Radio 4), *Rainbow* (Thames TV) and *Jackanory* (BBC), and he has also written numerous original plays which have been staged for radio, TV and theatre across the UK.

He has worked as a Director in BBC Children's Television, producer in BBC Schools Radio and BBC Radio Drama, Programme Controller of a commercial radio station, and Production Director and editor for an audio production company.

Michael has also served as the Chairman of The Children's Film Unit, Chairman of Factotum Theatre Company and on the board of The Attic Theatre, Wimbledon.

He is a Life Member of The Writers' Guild of Great Britain.

Michael's books include short story collection *My Village in the Valley*, and memoir *Out of the Blue*. He lives with his wife in Norfolk.